# Tempted by a SEAL

AN ALPHA SEALS NOVEL

Makenna Jameison

This book is a work of fiction. Names, characters, places, and incidents are the product of the author's imagination. Any resemblance to actual events, locales, or persons, living or dead, is coincidental.

Copyright © 2017 by Makenna Jameison

All rights reserved, including the right of reproduction in whole or in part in any form.

ISBN: 9781729033692

## ALSO BY MAKENNA JAMEISON

### ALPHA SEALS

SEAL the Deal
SEALED with a Kiss
A SEAL's Surrender
A SEAL's Seduction
The SEAL Next Door
Protected by a SEAL
Loved by a SEAL
Tempted by a SEAL
Married to a SEAL

### SOLDIER SERIES

Christmas with a Soldier
Valentine from a Soldier
In the Arms of a Soldier
Return of a Soldier
Summer with a Soldier

# Table of Contents

| | |
|---|---:|
| Prologue | 1 |
| Chapter 1 | 8 |
| Chapter 2 | 21 |
| Chapter 3 | 35 |
| Chapter 4 | 58 |
| Chapter 5 | 74 |
| Chapter 6 | 85 |
| Chapter 7 | 100 |
| Chapter 8 | 111 |
| Chapter 9 | 122 |
| Chapter 10 | 130 |
| Epilogue | 139 |
| Author's Note | 143 |
| About the Author | 145 |

# Prologue

Emma Williams glanced around the crowded bazaar in Kabul, tucking her long, flaming red hair more securely beneath her headscarf. Perspiration dampened the back of her neck as she took in the sights and sounds of the open market, and she cursed the thick hair she'd hidden. The clothing covering practically every inch of her skin.

She didn't exactly blend in with the locals though, and with her fair, porcelain skin and bright hair, she stood out amongst the Afghanis even more than most Westerners.

And there was no need to draw any further attention to herself.

The smell of kabobs seasoned with fresh herbs filled the warm air, drifting throughout the marketplace, and she watched a man animatedly talking as he sold several plates of them to a family.

The long, tunic-style blouse she had on over her

worn-in jeans fluttered in the slight breeze, and she would've killed for a breezy little sundress. Good heavens, even shorts and a tank top. Nothing like being covered from head to toe in the sweltering, 95-degree weather—well, not literally head to toe, she thought with a smirk.

She was wearing sandals.

But she looked exactly like every other Western aid worker here in Afghanistan—had blended in nicely with them for the past week and a half.

Never mind that she was really in the country conducting archeology research for the latest academic paper she was writing. Some of the locals might frown on a woman doing a "man's" job, but aid workers were welcome here—as long as they didn't reveal any skin, avoided all forms of alcohol, kept their hair covered, and never spent any time alone with a man.

Good heavens.

She respected the customs of other countries, but there was no way on Earth she could ever live here for an extended period of time, research or not.

"Look at those," her colleague Lily said, pointing toward another merchant's wares.

The dusty street they were walking along was lined up and down with vendors—booth after booth was filled with spices, traditional Afghani clothing, scarves, jewelry, and fresh fruits and vegetables. Colorful, woven tapestries fluttered in the slight breeze, and Emma's eyes were drawn to the tables of painted pottery that Lily was pointing to.

Some of the vases would look fabulous on an end table at her flat back in London, but it would be difficult to transport them safely back in her rush to leave in the morning.

Guilt seeped through her at the thought of leaving her colleagues and friend, but she didn't exactly have any other options.

"Beautiful," Emma agreed. "I'd probably break them on the flight back though."

Lily laughed, her light brown waves peeking out from her own headscarf. "You're here six months, right? I'm sure you can figure out how to safely pack them in your suitcase by then. Just wrap them up in your clothes or buy one of those gorgeous tapestries. I'm thinking of getting one for my apartment back home."

Emma smiled, nodding slightly at her American friend. Emma had gone through a painstaking process to obtain the necessary visas and paperwork to come to Afghanistan posing as an aid worker. Her friend was here for legitimate reasons—to actually help the people of this country. To work here for the duration of her visa.

But after the information Emma had accidentally uncovered this week?

She shuddered despite the heat.

No. She absolutely needed to return to London as quickly as possible.

Her eyes swept across the bazaar, making sure there was nothing out of the ordinary. Double checking to ensure she wasn't being followed.

Yes. She had to go back to London. It would be safer for everyone that way.

A group of men talking loudly by one stall in the market caught her attention, and she neatly turned around, walking in another direction as her pulse pounded and adrenaline surged through her veins.

Fear clutched her chest, and her eyes scanned the crowd mingling there.

She took a deep breath as she quickly hurried away, leaving Lily behind her.

They most certainly weren't the men one of her other colleagues had said were asking about her yesterday.

They couldn't be.

The market was filled with people, young and old, foreigners and locals alike, and she was letting her imagination get carried away.

It was bad enough she'd already drawn unwanted attention to herself. Gossip spread like wildfire about foreigners here, especially Western women, and the last thing she needed was more prying eyes. She'd snooped where she shouldn't have while conducting her research a few days ago, and it apparently hadn't gone unnoticed.

"Wait up!" Lily called out, hurrying after her.

"I just remembered something I have to pick up," Emma said, glancing back toward Lily's flushed face. Her eyes trailed back to the group of men again, and she picked up the pace. "Meet you in ten minutes by the fruit stalls?"

"Oh, sure," Lily said, looking confused as she fell in step beside Emma. "I thought you wanted to look at the tapestries with me."

"I will. I just need to purchase something else first."

"More tea?" Lily joked.

"They're certainly a people after my own heart," Emma said, relaxing slightly the further they walked.

"Not mine. They're aren't nearly enough coffee shops here in Kabul."

"You Americans and your coffee," Emma teased. "I don't think I'll ever get used to you drinking that harsh, bitter brew first thing in the morning."

Lily laughed. "Give me a few weeks. I'll change your mind."

"Highly unlikely. I'm a true Brit, born and bred. I'll meet you back by the fruit stalls in a few minutes," she said, pausing in the middle of the bazaar. "We can select a tapestry then if you like."

"All right," Lily agreed. "I'll meet you then. Catch ya later."

Emma watched her friend walk away before turning and continuing in the opposite direction. Having no intention of returning.

If those men she'd seen were the ones who'd been asking about her, there was no sense in dragging Lily into her problems. No point in potentially putting her in harm's way. It was better that Emma had ducked out of sight before they spotted her.

Lily would no doubt wonder where she was when she didn't show up in ten minutes, but if it meant keeping her safe? It was quite worth the secrecy and any hurt feelings that might ensue.

Emma shifted her tan leather backpack from one shoulder to the other, her stomach fluttering with nerves as she thought of the documents she'd discovered during her research the other day that were stuffed into the lining. She was catching a flight out tomorrow, and if she could just continue acting as if everything was normal for the next twenty-four hours, she'd be back in London in no time.

She had several academic journals interested in her research and was quite looking forward to some quiet time alone her materials, laptop, and a hot cup of tea.

And as for the documents she'd discovered?

A trip to the police would be in order as soon as she returned to London—or perhaps MI6. But it's not like she could just waltz in there announcing she'd found what looked to be a list full of targets for a terrorist attack. The guards certainly wouldn't let her just stroll into headquarters unannounced proclaiming she had that type of information. They probably wouldn't even believe her.

Perhaps some of her colleagues at the museum had government contacts she could reach out to. Officials who would believe the documents she'd found and insist on seeing them as soon as possible.

Certainly going to the police was necessary at the bare minimum.

Worry churned through her stomach.

Ducking between two booths, she set her backpack on the dusty ground and lifted a vase up to carefully inspect it. Maybe she should purchase one after all and stuff the papers she'd found into it. Her backpack seemed too obvious of a hiding spot.

But what if the vase broke?

Anyone who saw it would certainly notice what she'd hidden.

Wonder why she'd stuffed papers in there.

She tapped the vase with her fingertips, trying to determine how sturdy it might be, the gold band around her left ring finger glinting in the afternoon sunlight—you couldn't be too careful as a woman traveling alone in certain areas of the world.

If the locals believed she was a married woman, then she was all for a little white lie.

A young boy working alongside his family in the booth smiled up at Emma.

"Buy for 1,200 afghanis."

"No, thank you," she said, politely shaking her head.

"Yes?" he asked.

She shook her head no again and bent to pick up her backpack from the ground, uneasiness suddenly prickling across her skin. Her heart raced as the boy's gaze shifted to something behind her, a confused look on his face.

Swallowing nervously, Emma drew in a breath and turned to find two of the men who'd been arguing loudly standing before her.

Eyeing her with interest.

Startled, she took a step backward as icy cold fear raced down her spine.

Had they been following her around the bazaar?

One reached out toward her, and she couldn't follow the quickly flowing words coming from his mouth. His hand brushed against the backpack she was clutching.

She turned, knocking over the table of vases, listening to the shouts of the men and family behind her.

She ran.

# Chapter 1

Navy SEAL Hunter "Hook" Murdock grimaced as he took a swig of the lukewarm soda, muttering a curse under his breath. He shifted on his barstool, irritation seeping through him as laughter and conversations filled the air around him. He wasn't normally one to crave an ice-cold Coke, but damn. What the hell did the Brits have against ice cubes anyway?

He had half a mind to ask for a pint instead, but he never drank on the job.

And this one was just getting started.

Sweeping his gaze across the crowded pub, he caught his reflection in the mirror behind the bar—dark, shortly cropped hair that was just starting to look scruffy, the one-week-old growth of beard leftover from his latest op, the hint of an anchor tattoo on his bicep peeking out beneath his sleeve, and a second tattoo of a snake curling up his muscled forearm.

As if his appearance wasn't enough, the scowl on his face scared off most people.

If he wanted the company of a beautiful woman for the night, he could turn on the charm like the best of them—flash a smile, flex his biceps. Whisper a few meaningless words about how beautiful she was.

Not that he'd be picking up a woman in the middle of conducting surveillance.

His eyes scanned the noisy pub again, filling with Londoners after a day's work. Suit jackets were coming off. Sleeves getting pushed up. The greasy smell of fish and chips permeated the air, glasses clinked behind the bar as orders were rushed to be filled, and his stomach rumbled.

Damn he was hungry. But food could come later.

The young female bartender walked back over to him, leaning against the bar so that he could see the cleavage spilling out of her low-cut top. "Can I get you anything else, love?"

"How about a cup full of ice?"

She laughed, her breasts bobbing up and down as she stood. "You Americans."

He bristled as she walked away to help another customer. Maybe he could just wear a damn American flag to draw even more attention to himself.

Jesus Christ.

Most of his SEAL team was on a C-17 transport plane back to the States after conducting their latest op in the Middle East—rescuing the daughter of an American Senator who'd been taken hostage. Hunter's Delta SEAL team had joined the Alpha SEALs from Naval Amphibious Base Little Creek to conduct the rescue mission. The two teams made an intimidating show of force and were among the best of the best—elite, highly trained, and heavily armed. Although one of the SEALs had been injured, the op had otherwise gone off as planned.

Patrick "Ice" Foster, the leader of the Alpha SEALs, had been laid up in a hospital in Landstuhl, Germany but was finally back in Virginia on the road to recovery. He'd even gotten engaged to his girlfriend after the incident.

Ice was engaged. Imagine that.

Crazy what the threat of imminent death could lead a man to do.

Not that Hunter had anyone waiting for him back home.

Or that he wanted anyone to be.

Hunter's gut had churned as he'd watched the other SEAL team load onto the Black Hawks outside the terrorist camp in Afghanistan with Ice's limp body being dragged by two of the other men. That type of shit was something no one wanted to see.

Hunter and his Delta team had provided cover, sweeping the perimeter of camp as they shot at stray insurgents. Watching the other team get the fuck out of dodge.

Between the two SEAL teams, they'd taken out multiple terrorists as they infiltrated the camp. Come under heavy fire. Rescued the American hostage.

But that didn't lessen his taste for revenge.

Or his need to track down any and all others affiliated with the terror group.

The latest intelligence from the Pentagon indicated another woman may have been taken hostage—a British archeologist who'd gone to Afghanistan to conduct research. She'd been able to enter the country posing as an aid worker but hadn't been heard from in several days. Her American colleague had reported she'd never returned to the aid group's housing after they'd gotten separated at a market in Kabul.

The latest SITREP, or situation report of an unfolding incident, indicated the archeologist's suspected kidnapping may have been orchestrated by a couple of British citizens who'd turned over her information for a pretty penny—make that a pretty pound in this case.

He smirked.

Hunter had been in London on R&R when word from the Pentagon came in about the terrorists' ties to Kensington. He'd abandoned his plans to finish sight-seeing and flirting with British women during his much-needed time off and had set up shop in a hotel down the street.

He'd gone over the descriptions of the suspects this morning and received intelligence on their routines for the remainder of the day. It wasn't the typical job of a Navy SEAL, but hell, he'd been in the right place at the right time.

And just coming off an op connected to these bastards made him that much more inclined to hunt them down. The fact that they may have taken another innocent woman sent his protective instincts soaring and adrenaline surging through his veins.

Although he certainly enjoyed his time alone with the fairer sex—preferably beneath the covers—the fact that some terrorist assholes had tried to kidnap another woman sent rage roaring through him.

Best case scenario was that it was all a mistake—just because she hadn't been heard from didn't mean she'd been kidnapped.

But worst case?

He clenched his fists, mind swirling with the possibilities of where she was, when the barstool beside him was suddenly pulled back.

His fellow SEAL team member Mason "Riptide" Ryan sank down beside him, his cropped blond hair damp from a shower and eyes glinting in amusement as he took in the lukewarm drink in front of Hunter.

"Don't say it," Hunter muttered.

"I'm going to buy you a whole damn block of ice when we're back in the states."

"Doesn't help me much now, wise guy."

"Ain't that the truth."

"So much for a little R&R this week," Hunter said, cracking his knuckles. "I've had exactly one decent night's sleep. Not that I'm complaining about the woman I was with the other night," he added with a smirk. His gaze slid to a group of women laughing nearby, roaming over their curves, then swept back to Mason.

He had work to do.

Mason chuckled. "Yep. It's not exactly ideal to come right off one op and then get sucked back into this clusterfuck. Although how you managed to get us involved is beyond me. You'd think the Brits would be all over this."

Hunter smirked. "What can I say? I've got friends in high places. I'd rather deal with these assholes myself after rescuing the Senator's daughter," he said in a low voice.

"Damn straight," Mason agreed. "The poor girl looked scared out of her mind."

"Unfortunately, our hands are tied aside from

gathering intel though. After we get what we need, confirmation that these two assholes were involved, you can paint the town, pretty boy."

"I'm still wiped out from last night."

"What time did you drag your ass back to the hotel?"

"Three a.m. The British babe I met lived clear on the other side of London. I got lost on the damn Tube coming back."

Hunter guffawed. "You can pinpoint a location anywhere in the world within millimeters using GPS coordinates and sat imagery but can't figure out a damn subway system?"

"Hell, I was thinking with my dick the entire way to her place. She could've taken me across the goddamn English Channel, and I probably wouldn't have noticed. Besides, after three rounds between the sheets, I was wiped. And don't worry—she was fully satisfied as well. If nothing, I'm a gentleman."

The edge of Hunter's mouth quirked up. "Why didn't you wait and leave until morning then, Romeo?"

Mason chuckled. "Not my MO, man. Yours either."

Hunter smirked, shaking his head. "Touché."

Their entire Delta SEAL team was full of single, rough and tumble Alpha males who enjoyed the company of a beautiful woman. Whenever they were back stateside, they'd prowl around the Virginia Beach area, not far from their base in Little Creek, looking for a pretty woman to take home for the night.

Something about sunshine, sand, and beautiful women in bikinis did it every time.

Hunter had no desire to settle down with one woman—not when the whole damn world was his oyster. And hell if he didn't love diving for pearls.

Driving a woman wild in bed was his specialty—and if he could enjoy the pleasure of a different woman every weekend, he damn well would. No sense in tying himself down when he deployed all the time anyway. Nothing like trying to maintain a relationship when you couldn't say where you were going, what you were doing, or when you'd be back.

Most women he'd met couldn't handle a situation like that—and hell if life wasn't easier this way.

His SEAL team made an imposing force when they were together—even out of uniform, their shortly cropped hair, muscles, and certain swagger seemed to give away their profession.

And hell.

They were never short on ladies looking to spend the night with a Navy SEAL.

He'd already enjoyed a one-night-stand his first night in London—a university student he'd met while sightseeing. She'd asked if he was lost, and he'd gone along with it, figuring he'd seem less intimidating to her that way. Never mind that he'd memorized the map of the London streets and knew the exact way back to his hotel. Could practically count the number of steps from the street corner to the front door.

She'd batted those long lashes at him, and he'd gone along for the ride.

And ride him she had—all damn night.

Cowgirl. Reverse cowgirl. She was insatiable in bed—not that he'd had any complaints.

Hell, it was hard to remember the last time he'd enjoyed himself so much with a woman. She knew he was an American here visiting and wasn't expecting more than one night with him.

Knew that he'd literally be across the ocean in a few days.

And damn if that didn't make it even more enjoyable that way.

There was no need to let her down easy the next morning when they'd both known it was a one-time deal.

Hell.

They'd even had a quickie in the shower before they'd parted ways.

She'd screamed so loud as he'd made her come, he'd practically expected the British police to break down the hotel door.

"What are you smiling about?" Mason asked, ordering a soda.

"With ice!" Hunter called out to the bartender as she walked away.

Mason smirked.

"No thanks needed," Hunter said smoothly. "How the Brits drink their soda practically lukewarm is beyond me."

"You blokes need a pint," a young guy beside them said, chuckling as he took his own beer and headed over to his group of friends.

Hunter shook his head. "Tell me about it."

"He's right," Mason said, rubbing his hands together. "Let's get this show on the road so we can hightail it out of here."

"Gotta wait for the perps to make an appearance first. Soon as we get confirmation that they have info on the missing woman, we're outta here."

"You think they sold her out to the terror group?"

"I don't know damn well what to think. But most women don't travel to Afghanistan alone and then simply disappear. Her colleagues were the ones who went to the American Embassy when they didn't hear from her. Apparently, they notified the Brits."

"Shit. That stuff is fucked up."

"Roger that. Be right back," Hunter muttered, pushing his barstool back as he stood up.

Mason raised his eyebrows. "Spot a woman you fancy?"

"Gonna hit the head."

Mason smirked. "I'll keep an eye out."

"For the men or a woman?"

"Yep."

Hunter grunted in amusement before sauntering across the pub toward the bathroom. A waitress walked by carrying a tray of sizzling burgers and fries—make that chips—and his stomach rumbled. He hadn't eaten since lunch but could grab some food after they'd gotten eyes and ears on the men.

It was a damn fucking shame he couldn't take those assholes out himself, but it wouldn't exactly go unnoticed if he got into a fight in the middle of a crowded pub. His eyes swept around the area once more, and he nearly missed running into a beautiful redhead rushing the other way.

She was petite, barely coming up to his shoulder, and her fair skin and striking green eyes immediately drew his attention. Not to mention the swell of her breasts beneath the form-fitting, pink cashmere sweater she had on. The soft top hugged her curves enticingly, leaving little to the imagination. The fact that it fit her like a glove, yet didn't reveal any skin, was intriguing. Normally he was all about short skirts and low-cut tops, but on her? An innocent sweater had never looked so sexy.

"Pardon me," she said in a smooth British accent, her silky red hair spilling around her shoulders and her intoxicating floral scent filling the air.

"Ma'am," he said, his fingers just grazing her forearm to steady her.

"You're American," she said in surprise, pulling her arm away.

He quirked a brow. "How could you tell that from one word?"

Hell, if he didn't already miss the feel of her delicate arm beneath his fingers. He wanted to run his hands all over that soft cashmere and feel her soft, feminine curves beneath it. Trace his thumb over those full pink lips. Crowd into her space and pull her close.

"It's not common in England. Besides, most English men I know aren't nearly as tall as you. And they wouldn't go about manhandling me that way."

Hunter guffawed. "You almost fell over when you ran into me. Where's the fire? The way you were tearing through here there must be one somewhere."

"I most certainly did not run into you," she said haughtily.

"And what's preferable to 'ma'am' anyway? Would 'princess' work for you?"

"To be perfectly clear, you almost ran into me," she corrected him, her green eyes sparking. "You were looking around, probably at some other woman, like a typical man, and nearly plowed into me."

Hunter smirked. Hell yeah he'd love to plow into her—probably not in the manner she meant though.

"My apologies from preventing you from falling

flat on your face."

"That's the worst apology I've ever heard."

He crossed his arms. "That's because I don't have anything to apologize for."

"Excuse me," she huffed indignantly.

Her breasts just grazed against his bicep as she turned to slide by him, evidently ending the conversation, and his groin tightened. She was so damn soft, he couldn't help but imagine all those curves pressing up against him.

Her soft breasts rubbing against his muscular chest. Her small hands clinging to him as he claimed her. Her pink lips whispering in that sexy-as-fuck accent in his ear.

Why did British women seem so damn irresistible?

He loved the idea of some English chick whispering naughty words to him. It must be like the sexy librarian fantasy all guys had—some prim and proper looking, beautiful woman turning into a sex goddess when a man took her to bed.

Coming alive beneath his solid, muscular frame. Whimpering as he made her orgasm again and again. Begging him for mercy he penetrated her, drawing out her pleasure for as long as possible until she screamed out his name in surrender. Until her tight pussy clenched again and again around his throbbing cock.

Unable to resist, he glanced back over his shoulder, watching her sweet ass sashay back and forth as she walked away in those sexy-as-fuck tight jeans.

Hell, she was a looker.

And he couldn't resist one last taunt.

"American men are big all over, princess."

She looked back at him, her face flushing. He couldn't tell if it was in anger or arousal, but then she retorted, "Arrogant prick."

He chuckled, his eyes drifting lower to her heart-shaped ass, clad in that tight denim. Damn if he didn't want to have a closer inspection of those sweet curves.

Preferably without the jeans.

The woman he'd bedded the other night had some naughty lingerie on under her casual clothes. Did all British chicks wear stuff like that? Because he sure as hell might need to give up the Navy and become an Ex-Pat in London if that were the case.

Holy hell.

Forcing himself to look away, he continued toward the men's room and shoved open the door. He adjusted his earpiece a minute later when he re-emerged.

Mason's voice was suddenly in his ear, laughing.

"American men are big all over? Who gave you that Hallmark line?"

"It was damn poetic, right?" he asked. "Not sure why she didn't immediately wrestle me to the ground right then and have her wicked way with me."

"Yeah, in your dreams," Mason chuckled. "I've never seen a woman move so fast—in the opposite direction."

"I bet she's wild in bed. Redheads always are."

A few men sitting at a table beside him chuckled, and Hunter muttered a curse as he wove his way back through the growing crowd. He was drawing attention to himself all over the damn place.

By the time he'd crossed the pub back toward the bar where he'd been sitting, his gaze was drawn to movement outside.

Hunter's gaze narrowed as he saw two Middle Eastern men lingering on the sidewalk, animatedly talking with hand gestures. A woman walking by stepped away from them, frowning, and a beat passed before they turned and pushed open the pub's door.

Even amongst the after-work crowd they stood out.

Expensive suits. Slicked-back hair.

The shorter one carrying an expensive leather briefcase.

He'd memorized the photographs of the men he was seeking earlier. Knew every detail of their faces, from the small scar on the cheek of one to the angular jaw and slightly crooked nose on the other.

Bingo.

## Chapter 2

Emma's heart raced as she walked toward the crowded bar, her palms slick as she clutched her leather backpack in both hands. Unlike the adrenaline she'd had coursing through her over the past few hours, though, her pulse was pounding in an entirely different way at the moment.

Awareness prickled over her skin as she felt the heated gaze of the man she'd nearly run into watch her walk away, and she was certain her face was flushed.

The curse of being so fair skinned, she thought in exasperation.

She certainly wasn't *interested* in a man who'd bragged about the size of American men.

Good heavens.

American men were large all over?

There was certainly no doubt their egos were.

He was just cocky enough that he probably did

have the goods to match.

Not that she ever intended on finding out.

She had enough to worry about without drawing undue attention to herself anyhow. Without having foreign men hit on her in crowded pubs. She'd barely been back in London a day, and she was already in trouble again.

The jaded police officer she'd spoken to earlier had told her to go down to the station with her information. He hadn't seemed to understand or care about the documents she'd found. With the threat level in Britain at "severe," you'd think he'd have been more concerned. But it's not like she could wave them around in public where anyone could see.

She couldn't go back to her flat—not after the way it had been ransacked this afternoon. When her neighbor had texted her mobile and let her know the police were there and that the entire place had been overturned, she'd fled. She hadn't even gone back to investigate the damage or file a proper police report.

Not when she was being followed. When someone knew about the documents she had.

She was too afraid to even go to the police alone for fear of being caught. She didn't dare walk around in public alone when someone was clearly after her. When she'd nearly been grabbed a week ago in Kabul and someone had found her back in London.

Still, her heart raced unexpectedly as her mind lingered on her brief encounter with the American man, replaying every moment in slow motion. As heat bloomed across her skin.

The guy she'd bumped into had towered above her, with a week's worth of dark stubble on his strong jaw and multiple tattoos on his muscular arms. He was confident and arrogant. Brash. Practically oozing testosterone. A man like him was probably used to women dropping their knickers the moment he walked in. No doubt there were pounds of muscle beneath that soft, cotton tee-shirt he had on. And she'd felt his restrained strength as his fingers had grazed her forearm, as she'd brushed past him when she'd walked away.

A guy like him no doubt thoroughly knew his way around a woman's body. What was that expression her American friend Lily was so fond of? Sex on a stick?

Emma had felt small and almost fragile beside him. Feminine. And that was unexpected, because she was fiercely independent. Content doing things on her own. Although she dated from time to time, so was so busy with travel and her research, she didn't have time for a serious relationship. A commitment of any sort. She had her career to think of and refused to let a man stand in the way of her success. Not after everything she'd worked for.

No doubt he was here on a vacation anyhow, just visiting London, and she certainly wasn't looking to spend one night with a man she'd never see again.

Never mind that he'd smelled like clean soap and a hint of some spice—cologne maybe? Not aftershave since he clearly hadn't seen a razor recently. From his short, cropped dark hair to his broad shoulders and the way his jeans hung perfectly from narrow hips, everything about him was attractive.

Appealing.

Normally she was drawn to clean-cut men in button-down shirts and pressed trousers. The type of man who wouldn't dream of marking their body with ink and were well-educated and well-spoken. Academics, like her. Who had attended prestigious universities and had their work published in esteemed journals.

That guy looked like he'd spent the afternoon at the gym, showered, and thrown on the first pair of clean clothes he'd found. Popped into a pub and tried out a few chat-up lines at the first woman he noticed.

She shivered as she recalled his searing gaze on her. No doubt he was already chatting up another woman by now, and it was for the best.

Emma had enough other things to worry about.

Steeling her nerves, she slid onto an empty barstool at the crowded bar, determined to put the American guy out of her mind.

Glasses clanked around her as the bartender lined up clean cups, and patrons talked loudly above the music. The greasy scent of fish and chips filled the air—so different than the open bazaar in Kabul. It had been only a week but felt like a lifetime ago—in that short span of time, her entire world had turned upside down.

But she was safe at the moment.

Unnoticed in the crowded pub.

The man seated beside her had his gaze on a laughing group of young women nearby. There was an empty barstool with a drink beside him, so his buddy or girlfriend was probably on his or her way back. And she was perfectly content to be left alone.

"Gin and tonic, please," she said to the bartender.

"Coming right up."

The woman flipped her white cloth over her shoulder and moved toward the bottles of spirits, laughing with a couple of young men seated at the bar as she made Emma's drink.

Emma warily scanned the crowd.

A moment later, she released a breath she hadn't even realized she'd been holding, allowing her backpack to rest between her feet on the stool's perch. Her shoulders and neck were tight with tension, and she absentmindedly brushed her hair back over her shoulders.

Tried to relax.

To think of a plan.

Visiting friends in London was out of the question—there was no need to draw any of them into danger. Not until she had this whole thing sorted.

Maybe she should just ring the police and ask them to meet her here. Tell them her flat was ransacked and she'd been too scared to return.

But it's not like they'd just swing by the pub to take her statement—not unless there was an actual emergency. She should've turned over the papers to the authorities the moment she'd landed in Heathrow yesterday—rid herself of the situation altogether.

Now someone was literally hunting her down—there was no chance it was merely a coincidence her flat had been torn apart. Not within twenty-four hours since she'd returned. Not with the information she had.

A gin and tonic suddenly appeared before her, and Emma realized she'd been so lost in thought she hadn't even noticed the bartender's return. She took a sip, realizing she needed to be more aware of her surroundings. Careful with who she spoke to.

It probably wasn't even safe sitting here for long.

She needed to move. Make sure she handed over

the information through the proper channels—found someone who'd believe the documents she'd accidentally discovered.

She couldn't let her guard down for even a moment.

Lifting her gaze, her stomach flipped as she saw the man she'd run into earlier heading in her direction.

\*\*\*

Hunter strode across the pub, fists clenched, watching as the two men sat down at a table not far from him, completely unaware of his presence.

Jesus fucking Christ.

He felt his phone vibrating in the pocket of his pants but ignored it, his gaze trained on the two men.

If those two assholes had turned over an innocent woman for cash, he'd fucking read them the riot act himself. Forget following his chain of command and calling in the Brits to make an arrest—he'd end them himself, consequences be damned.

Just as soon as he determined the missing woman's location.

His blood boiled at the thought of an innocent woman being held captive. It was bad enough that his SEAL team had just tracked down the Senator's daughter—luckily, she'd been unharmed, but a Western woman being held hostage in the Middle East wouldn't usually be so lucky. Maybe the latest victim wasn't American, but that didn't mean she'd be safe from those bastards—rape, torture. Other unspeakable acts.

His jaw clenched as his mind raced through

varying scenarios.

The fact that the pub was filling up worked to his advantage. He side-stepped a couple walking up to the bar and surreptitiously planted a receiver on the back of one of the men's chairs and he strode by.

He'd be able to hear every damn word they said.

After Hunter collected the details he needed from the men's conversation, namely confirmation they'd been involved with the kidnapping of the missing archeologist, he and Mason would be on a flight back to the States.

Maybe even sent back out on an op to retrieve her.

It would just fucking kill him to leave those assholes here, untouched.

He had no idea what his next assignment would be though.

His SEAL team deployed all over the world, at Uncle Sam's beck and call 24/7. Hunter had joined the Navy fresh out of high school and served his country for fifteen years. Watching the twin towers fall on 9/11 had cemented his career in the military. Same with many of the guys he served with.

At thirty-three, he'd given nearly half his life to the service. To tracking down low-life scum on all corners of the world—Drug lords. Terrorists. Arms dealers. Human traffickers.

He'd seen shit no one should ever have to. Slept in places he wouldn't wish on his worst enemy. But he'd been damn proud to serve his country. To help the weak and innocent.

Guys like him weren't made for a desk job anyway. He needed to be moving. Training. Fighting alongside his men.

If giving up his R&R this week served the greater

good, then so be it.

He'd signed over his life to his country years ago.

Hunter did a double-take as he sank back onto his barstool a moment later, the beautiful redhead perched only a few feet away. Mason's gaze was flicking back and forth between the men Hunter had just bugged and two young women in slim fitting skirts and button-down blouses that hugged their full breasts.

Hunter smirked and cocked his head, and Mason nodded, nonchalantly glancing over at the men they'd been tracking.

"Those two idiots didn't even see you walk by," Mason commented.

"Works to our advantage that way."

"Let's hope they're feeling talkative."

"Yep. Doubt they'll announce where our missing woman is though."

"So what? Now you followed me over to the bar?" the beautiful redhead asked in her smooth British accent, her green eyes flashing in irritation as she looked over at Hunter. She crossed her denim-clad legs, a leather backpack resting at her feet on the stool's perch. "In case you didn't catch on earlier, I'm not interested."

Hunter raised his eyebrows, taking in her pink lips and slightly flushed cheeks. With her fair skin, even the slightest shade of pink showed up immediately. Enticingly.

Her silken red hair hung past her shoulders, just touching the swells of her gorgeous breasts. As she lifted a glass to her mouth, he tried not to smile as he watched her take a sip. This woman looked sexy no matter what she did.

And damn it all to hell, he had work to do.

"I was sitting here earlier," he said coolly. "Maybe you were the one stalking my friend and me? Decided to come sit by him and wait for me to return?"

"Stalking? It rather looks like you chased me over here—all the way across the pub, I might add."

"Mason Ryan," Mason said, extending a hand. "We'd love for you to join us."

The redhead looked momentarily startled at his interruption but extended her hand as well.

"Emma," she said, without offering her last name. "And no thank you. I'm quite fine here on my own."

Alarm bells began going off in Hunter's head as she lifted her backpack up to her lap, her fingers clutching it tightly.

Emma.

Funny that she had the same name as the missing archeologist. But that was probably a common British name. And the missing woman was exactly that—missing. Not sitting in a pub in London glowering at him.

Looking sexier than any woman had a right to.

"Don't worry about him," Mason said easily, cocking his head toward Hunter. "He's always in a bad mood."

"I can imagine. Are you sure that you want to spend your evening in his company?"

Hunter smirked and surreptitiously adjusted his earpiece, listening in on the men's conversation. Interestingly enough, Emma seemed annoyed that he hadn't introduced himself yet, her searing gaze flickering his way. The pout on her lips was cute as hell though.

What was that expression? The lady doth protest

too much?

At this rate, he and Mason were going to have to move if they wanted to concentrate and get their job done. He winked at Emma but glanced back over toward the men, keeping an eye on their movements.

A hint of a blush crept over her cheeks again, and he cleared his throat.

"No one's forcing you to sit there, princess. But I have to admit, I don't mind. Didn't mind when you bumped into me earlier, either."

"I already said—"

"Are you from London?" Mason asked. "Maybe you can show us around later. Tell us the best places to hang out. I got lost on the damn subway system last night."

"Not originally, but I work here now. And I'm sure you can convince some other woman into showing you two around the city."

"Fair enough," Mason said with a smile. "So what do you do?"

Emma seemed to relax slightly, but the men Hunter was listening to were animatedly talking now, and he narrowed his gaze in concentration, occasionally stealing a glance her way.

"Why don't you tell me about yourself first?"

Mason shrugged. "Not much to tell. I'm in the U.S. military—same with Hunter, here. We're on a vacation of sorts—R&R."

"And you decided to come to London?"

"We were flying back from a deployment," he said without elaborating.

Although the woman seemed innocent enough, there was no need to go around advertising in the middle of a British pub that both of them were Navy

SEALs. They couldn't exactly hide the fact when they were back in Little Creek, but in Europe? Letting her know they were U.S. military was more than enough.

Especially considering they'd never see her again.

"And you're the only two men in the pub who ordered a soda instead of a pint?" she asked, brushing some of that long, red hair back behind her shoulders. "Seems somewhat strange, doesn't it?"

Her hair fell back into place, a strand teasing the swell of one breast again, and Hunter's groin tightened.

He suddenly imagined her riding him in bed—her flaming red hair wild as she bucked on top of him, those soft, full breasts bouncing up and down, her mouth forming a perfect "o" as she cried out in pleasure.

Hell.

He'd been with a hundred women.

What was so special about her?

She was sexy as hell but far too observant for her own good.

"We've got a strict training regimen," Mason explained. "So are you going to tell us what you do, or do I have to guess? Model maybe? Trapeze artist?"

Her gaze flickered over to Hunter.

"You're awfully quiet considering you were nothing but talk earlier," she said in her smooth British accent.

Hell.

Got him every time.

No sense in telling her he'd bugged a nearby table and was currently conducting surveillance of two operatives who possibly had ties to terrorists in the Middle East. Or that she was probably in over her head just by sitting here beside them.

"Quite observant, aren't you?" he asked, raising an eyebrow. "Especially since you've told me several times you're not interested."

His mouth quirked up as she flinched.

"Like Mason already said, we're military. U.S. Navy. We're just here in London for a few days on R&R. Might as well see the sights while we're in town. And what do you do aside from looking gorgeous while following men around pubs?"

She flushed, much to his amusement, the slight pink on her cheeks arousing as hell. Hunter imagined she'd look like that as she came—with all her fair skin, she'd probably flush all over. Her cheeks, her breasts.

Damn shame he wouldn't ever find out.

The two men he was watching were wasting a hell of a long time talking about the food and beer. By the time he heard anything of relevance, Emma would probably be long gone.

Just like the supposed missing British archeologist.

"I had no idea you were sitting here," Emma said, looking affronted. "I came into the pub to order a drink like everyone else."

Hunter's ears perked up as the men finally began talking about the matter at hand.

"They don't know what happened to her," one of the men said in a thick accent. "She was located in a bazaar in Kabul but then vanished."

He clenched his fist.

Vanished?

What the fuck?

"How the hell could she simply disappear?" the other man asked. "Weren't several men tracking her?"

"Somehow she escaped."

The other man bit out a curse. "She has the documents we need. See this?" he asked.

Hunter's gaze flicked back to the table, where the two men looked at some papers. "Two pages are missing. We find her, and we retrieve what we need. She can't have that information."

"They were fucking supposed to handle this."

"They didn't. It's possible she's on her way back to London."

"We'll find her. Do you have a picture?"

"Of the woman? Yes. She's quite beautiful. Pity she escaped."

Hunter narrowed his gaze, exchanging a confused glance with Mason.

"Doesn't sound right," Mason said in a low voice, pulling out his phone. "I'll contact the CO and see if we missed something."

Hunter nodded, his gaze landing on Emma again. If the missing woman had escaped yet no one had heard from her, then where the hell was she? Were they following the wrong lead?

And why was this chick in the pub acting so damn mysterious?

"I can see you're not even paying attention," Emma said, swirling the ice cubes around in her glass. She took a sip of her drink, and he watched as she swallowed, enjoying his view of the long, slender column of her throat. The soft cashmere that hugged her breasts as his gaze dropped lower. "Spot another woman you fancy?"

Hunter's took in her wide green eyes, flushed cheeks, and full, pink lips.

Fucking beautiful.

Emma.

But it couldn't be. The name was just a coincidence.

"I'm all ears, princess," he said, his voice gruff. "You seem reluctant to share anything about yourself. Maybe you usually just sit around your castle all day? I'm sure you could convince plenty of British guys to wait on you hand and foot. Seems like it'd get boring after a while though."

"Princess? Not hardly. And I certainly don't 'sit around' all day doing nothing."

He cocked a brow, watching as she smirked at him, her green eyes sparking. Hell if he didn't love a woman who was a challenge. Not that he had time to play games.

"Another soda?" the female bartender asked, leaning up against the bar again. Her gaze flicked back and forth between Hunter and Emma, amusement filling her eyes.

Annoyed by the interruption, Hunter gruffly said no.

Emma flipped her red hair over her shoulders again in what was clearly a practiced move. He wouldn't mind running his fingers through all that softness. Finding out if she tasted as delicious as she looked.

She cleared her throat, sounding as prim and proper and British as she had when she'd first bumped into him. "If you really must know, I'm an archeologist."

Hunter's stomach dropped.

# Chapter 3

Emma calmly took a sip of her gin and tonic and tried to ignore the palpitations in her heart as piercing blue eyes bore into her. As Hunter's hand, resting on top of the bar, clenched into a fist. The tattoo of a snake curling up his forearm was somehow both intimidating and enticing. As was all that corded muscle beneath his skin.

He was gruff and macho, but all that strength wrapped up in tanned, toned, flesh?

Hotter than hell.

As were his broad shoulders, muscled chest, and thick biceps.

The stubble covering his strong jaw.

After the week she'd had, the last thing she needed was a macho American military guy following her around the pub and hitting on her.

Asking too many questions.

Making her stomach do flips any time he looked

her way.

At the moment, all she needed was to calm her nerves with a drink or two while she figured out her next move. While she determined just how deeply in trouble she actually was. Certainly she should be able to make it to the police station. How many men could actually be after her?

Her gaze slid to her brown leather backpack, now resting on her lap. The documents she'd found in Afghanistan were there, as well as backup copies on a thumb drive she'd carefully sewn into the lining.

Look at her—so damn domestic.

Sewing.

She'd laugh if the situation wasn't so out of control and beyond anything she could've imagined.

And when she'd ducked into the pub earlier because she was certain she was being followed, she'd nearly run into the first person who'd crossed her path. A man who was now perched two barstools away from her, looking dangerous and sexy and too damn attractive for his own good.

The guy she was seated beside seemed harmless enough—tan, blond hair, blue eyes. He probably lived on a beach somewhere in the US and went surfing every weekend. He looked muscular and fit. All American.

But just because he was military didn't mean he was used to dealing with the type of men who were after her.

Ruthless businessmen who'd turned her over to armed insurgents.

Who'd thought nothing of taking cash for an innocent woman.

She'd heard about the American woman who'd

been kidnapped a few weeks ago yet had been foolish enough to travel to Afghanistan anyway while conducting her research. Thinking that she'd be safe posing as an aid worker.

Assuming no one would notice when she'd snuck away from the others.

A chill raced down her spine at the memory of being grabbed from the streets. Nearly tossed in the back of a truck. She'd managed to escape and hide behind some of the booths in the market until nightfall, and she hadn't returned to the aid office where she worked.

She'd simply vanished.

"Are you all right?" Mason asked beside her, his expression concerned.

She realized she'd gone perfectly still, staring at her drink, as she thought back over the past week.

"Fine," she said, mustering up a smile. Forcing herself to glance around the crowded pub. She was safe here—safe from any outside threats, at least.

It was the man whose penetrating gaze kept sweeping her way that sent her heart skittering to a halt—Tall. Dark. Mysterious.

She didn't need a distraction like him right now.

Or ever.

"You're an archeologist?" he asked as he carefully watched her, his voice a deep rumble that sent shivers of a different sort racing down her spine.

"Yes, that's right. I studied at Oxford."

"I never introduced myself—Hunter Murdock," he said, reaching across Mason toward her.

Emma took his hand, and the feel of his large, slightly calloused hand wrapping around hers sent goosebumps across her flesh. Making her feel inexplicably safe.

Tendons bulged from his skin, and muscles twined up his thick forearm. His hand was rough but warm, and he held hers just a beat too long.

"Emma," she said, suddenly feeling foolish as she stared at him.

Reluctantly, she pulled away, not unaware of his fingertips just grazing across her skin as he let her go.

"Well, Emma Nolastname, you must not go digging around through ancient ruins Indiana Jones style—your hands are too soft."

She pressed her lips together, trying not to break into a smile. "I primarily do research now. My findings have been published in multiple academic journals around the world. But don't worry, I logged plenty of hours in the field back at university."

"Beauty and brains," Hunter quipped. "A dangerous combination."

He winked at her again, and she felt an unexpected surge of warmth wash over her skin as her heart pounded. She wasn't the type of woman to fall at a man's feet, but she had a feeling he could charm the pants off anyone.

Not that she planned on showing him her knickers.

Her face flamed at the thought, and she only hoped he didn't notice.

Right.

With her fair complexion, that was like asking someone not to notice the sun rising every morning.

"I do travel frequently for work, but I'm usually poring over research and documents, not digging up ancient artifacts. I'll admit the latter sounds far more interesting though. Probably makes for better stories at cocktail parties as well."

"How often do you travel?" he asked.

"Every month or so. It really just depends on what I'm working on at the moment and where I am in my research. Why do you ask?"

Hunter exchanged a glance with Mason, who looked up from texting someone on his mobile. "Just curious about something. Where was your last trip?"

"The Middle East," she said, not elaborating.

Her own mobile vibrated in her backpack, and she pulled it out, glancing down at the screen to see another text from her neighbor.

*A man was here looking for you earlier. Should I ring the police again?*

*I'm worried about you.*

Emma shoved her mobile into her backpack, swallowing. Maybe she should ditch the thing all together. If the men looking for her had found out where she lived, they could certainly find her mobile number. Track her using GPS or some other technology.

Coming back to London with the documents she'd discovered was a big mistake.

Piercing blue eyes met hers as she looked up. She scanned the chiseled planes of his face, the firm set of his jaw.

Hunter's eyes narrowed as his gaze fell on her backpack.

"I should get going," she said, suddenly climbing down from the barstool. "That was my neighbor—there's a problem at my flat."

"Emma," he said, nailing her with a gaze.

Her eyes were drawn to the earpiece she hadn't noticed before. To the way his eyes swept around the entire pub before once again meeting hers.

"Who are you?" she asked, her heart racing as sudden awareness seeped through her.

Loud laughter erupted from a group of men behind them, her head turning in their direction, and when she looked back toward Hunter and Mason, she was startled to see two Middle Eastern men seated at a table not far from them.

London was a huge, diverse city, with a population of nearly nine million people—but that didn't stop her from trembling as her eyes took in the scar on one man's cheek and the crooked nose of the other. As she recalled talking to them in the market in Kabul last week.

They'd blended in then, with traditional Afghani dress and beards.

But she'd recognize their faces anywhere.

"Shit," Mason said at the same moment Hunter was on his feet.

Mason adjusted something in his ear, and she realized both of them were listening in on something. Or to someone.

Holy crap. Were they somehow involved with the men who'd kidnapped her? Were they after her, too?

Hunter moved toward her as Mason headed in the opposite direction, Hunter's broad form blocking her view. He towered above her, his wide shoulders right in her line of vision as he gently wrapped his thick fingers around her forearm. "We have to get you out of here," he said, ducking low so that his head hovered near hers.

His clean, spicy scent filled the air between them as her heart pounded.

As she panicked and couldn't decide whether to

stay with him or run.

"But how—what? I'm not going anywhere with you."

"Those two men you're frightened of?" he asked, his voice gravel. "That's whose conversation we're listening in on. That's who just spotted you."

"You said you were in the military!" she accused, looking up at him. "What are you doing here in a London pub watching men like them?"

"We are," Hunter assured her. "It's long story. Which I'll explain after we get you out the back door."

"Why do I need to go out the back door?"

His blue eyes blazed. "Because they saw you. Mason is cutting them off. Now go!"

Emma gasped as Hunter crowded into her space, leaving her no choice but to step back.

Turn.

Run.

Her eyes scanned the pub, but everything else was normal—people laughing, throwing back drinks. The bartender sliding shots across the counter. More people coming in after work for a drink.

It was just her world that was unraveling around her.

She heard a table crashing to the ground behind her, men shouting. The sound of glass breaking.

Hunter's large hand spread across her back, jolting her back into the present as his warmth seeped into her. As his presence behind her calmed her racing mind.

"They spotted you, Princess. Now move!"

\*\*\*

Emma ran toward the emergency exit of the pub, the fire alarm sounding as she pushed open the heavy door. Hunter's large frame loomed behind her, shoving the door the rest of the way open with ease as they exited onto the busy, traffic-filled street.

It was beginning to drizzle in typical London fashion, the drab sky perfectly mirroring her feelings. She ran to the corner, a red double-decker bus following a stream of taxis driving by. Leave it to her to escape the men in the pub but be stopped by the damn London traffic.

Tourists snapped pictures from the bus at the commotion behind her, and she hastened a glance back. Hunter was right behind her, his intense gaze sweeping the area as other onlookers stopped. With his jaw taut and fists clenched, he looked ready to take on anything or anyone who might come after them.

Not that one man was a match for the ones that had tried to grab her in Kabul.

"What about your friend?" she asked. "He's still back in the pub!"

Patrons were now streaming out of the doors as the fire alarm blared, some of them still holding their drinks and laughing as if it were an everyday occurrence. Sirens sounded in the distance as more fat raindrops began to fall, the skies about to burst, and Emma brushed away one cold raindrop that landed on her cheek.

Hunter watched, looking unfazed as he stood there in his tee-shirt and cargo pants. Like he ran out of pubs every day with a woman he didn't know. Left his buddy behind to fight the bad guys.

His bicep flexed as he adjusted his earpiece once

again, the cotton of his tee-shirt stretching around the huge muscle.

Good heavens. She wasn't normally one to ogle a man, but this one was a sight to behold.

Too bad she had bigger problems to deal with.

"He's subdued them," Hunter said, his voice gruff. "Said to get the hell out of here."

"Both of them?"

Blue eyes flicked back to her. Blazed. "My men are well-trained. We've taken on much worse than those two fuck-ups—excuse my language. Mason can catch up with us later."

"Why were you listening in on their conversation?"

"No time to explain right now," he said, placing his hand on her lower back as he stepped closer. "There are other men involved. Other people who could be watching us right now. We need to get you out of sight."

She looked around frantically, as if the answer would somehow appear out of thin air. The rain began falling harder, quickly dampening her long hair and cashmere sweater. Leaving round water stains on the leather backpack she was still tightly clutching.

"Come on," Hunter said, guiding her across the street as the light changed. "I need to grab my gear from the hotel and we're outta here."

"I can't go back to my flat—they ransacked it earlier. My neighbor texted my mobile and said the entire place had been torn apart."

Hunter's jaw was set in a hard line as he glanced down at her. "Why didn't you say anything?"

"What? Why would I?" she asked, looking up at him and blinking as wet drops stuck to her lashes. "I don't even know you. I ducked into the pub because I thought someone was following me."

"And you were right," he quipped. "Come to my hotel."

"I'm not staying there with you."

"Nope. We're grabbing some stuff and leaving. If they're following you, the last thing I want is to be a sitting duck in a damn hotel room. Those men are far more dangerous than you know."

Emma chuffed out a laugh, coming to a halt in the middle of the sidewalk. "Are you serious? They nearly kidnapped me from a market in Kabul a week ago—I know exactly how dangerous they are. Those two men in the pub tried to sell me off to some foreigners. And what makes you think I trust you anyway? For all I know, you could be working with them."

Hunter nailed her with a glare, swiping the back of one large hand across his eyes to wipe away the rain. Tiny droplets of water still clung to his chiseled face. Dampened his dark hair. "I just hustled you out the back door and left my buddy there alone."

"You won't even tell me why you were there in the first place! Why should I believe a word that you say?"

"I'll explain later, princess. It's not safe here on the street. Now let's roll out."

Taking a deep breath, she reluctantly hurried along beside him, swinging her backpack onto her back and trying to keep up with his long strides.

A taxi driving through a puddle sent a spray of water splashing onto Hunter's cargo pants, and he muttered a curse, barely breaking his stride.

"Why are they after you?" he asked, his voice

gruff.

He suddenly grabbed his mobile from his pocket and glanced at the screen, frowning, as he tried to shield his device from the lingering rain with one hand.

"Is everything okay?"

"Damn peachy," he muttered, his eyes sweeping the surrounding area. "Just my CO updating me on some intel."

"Your CO?"

"The boss man."

Emma laughed despite herself, drawing another smirk from Hunter as his gaze once again locked with hers. She cleared her throat. "You want to know why they were after me? It turns out I discovered something they want back."

"Care to fill me in?"

"At the moment—no."

"You can trust me," he said, his voice gruff.

"You've given me no reason to."

The corner of his mouth quirked up. "Aside from hustling you out the door and ensuring your safety you mean?"

"Aside from that," she agreed.

He grumbled something unintelligible. "You want to know what I do? I'm a Navy SEAL. We were on our way back from an op and are here in London on R&R, just like I already said. And I happened to be in the right place at the right time and agreed to do a little off-the-books surveillance."

"On the two men in the pub?"

"Affirmative," he said. "That's my hotel right over there," he added, nodding at a building across the busy street. "I need to grab my stuff, and then we'll figure out our next move."

"We?" she asked, looking at him in confusion.

"I'm here to gain intel on those two men—if they're after you, that means you're involved too, princess."

"I don't like any of this."

Hunter chuffed out a laugh. "Neither do I. Not tracking down men affiliated with a terrorist group on my R&R—in the middle of goddamn London—not leaving Mason alone in the pub to fend for himself, and I sure the hell don't like the fact that you're wrapped up in all of this."

"You don't even know me," she protested.

"I'm a damn Navy SEAL. The definition of my career is helping people. I can't talk about specifics, but know this—I'd never let harm come to a woman. Never."

His jaw clenched in a hard line as she gazed up at him, and her exhaustion from the past week finally began to sink in as her adrenaline rush faded. She sniffed, blinking back tears, and looked warily toward his hotel.

Swallowed.

Hunter gaze shifted to her in surprise.

"I just don't know what to do—I don't have anywhere to go. I mean, it's not like I can drag my friends into this. And the men who are after me already found my flat."

"You'll come with me. It's already decided."

"Nothing's been decided."

"I have connections. You tell me what information you have, and we'll make sure it gets into the right hands. If it's enough for them to chase you all the way back from Afghanistan, it must be pretty damn important."

"But how will that stop them from coming after me?"

A shadow crossed his face. "It won't. But we'll figure it out."

***

Emma followed Hunter into the ornate lobby of the hotel, wrapping her arms around herself as she shivered. Nothing like a cold London downpour to dampen her spirits—no pun intended. Long, wet locks of hair stuck to her face, her drenched sweater clung to her like a second skin, and for a moment, she recalled the 95-degree heat in Afghanistan a week ago. The sticky perspiration on the back of her neck as she wandered through the bazaar.

Funny how she would've given anything then for a nice, cool London day.

She'd best be careful what she wished for though before she ended back up in the godforsaken place. Because if those men dragged her back, she certainly wouldn't be spending time in the market on a beautiful, sunny day.

She walked carefully across the oriental carpet of the hotel's lobby, eyeing the plush lounge chairs arranged around a low table. Wouldn't she love to sink into one for a moment—if only it wasn't in plain sight of the street and hundreds of people walking by.

Who knew who was watching them? Who else had been following her around London?

She'd rest later, when she figured out somewhere safe to go.

When she figured out if the man she was with was

someone she could trust.

She shuddered, Hunter's gaze sliding toward her as he punched a button for the elevator. "You cold?"

"I'll be fine."

"You're soaking wet," he said, his voice soft. "I have some clothes you can change into."

The elevator doors opened, and he glanced behind them, his eyes narrowing. Emma realized once again that she should be paying more attention. Should be watching everyone around her. Her gaze followed his, but she didn't see anything out of the ordinary—a couple strolling across the lobby, hand-in-hand. An Australian family checking in as their young toddler jumped up and down.

What did she expect? Someone to jump out from behind the rubbish bin and demand she hand over the documents?

Hunter gestured for her to go ahead, and she stepped onto the elevator, grateful to be out of sight. "I doubt your clothes would fit me anyhow," she commented. "You're quite a bit taller than me."

He jabbed at the elevator buttons for several different floors, the snake tattoo twisting on his muscled forearm as each number lit up, and she looked at him questioningly.

"Just in case anyone was watching for what floor we get off on. The display is above the elevators in the lobby, and I can't assume no one was watching."

"Right," she said faintly, feeling completely out of her element.

"And as for my clothes?" he said, cracking his knuckles as he appraised her. "I won't complain if you want to walk around naked, princess, but you don't seem like the type. I don't like the idea of you walking around shivering in wet clothes all night either, but be my guest if that's what you prefer."

She gave a faint laugh, tears smarting her eyes again.

"Hell," he muttered, running a hand through his damp hair.

His wet tee-shirt clung to his chest, and she could see the outline of every muscle. Broad pecs, rippling abs—the guy could be the model Michelangelo's David was chiseled from. Maybe he really was a Navy SEAL—what did she know about the American military anyway? It seemed quite strange that he'd be here in London listening in on conversations to men who had terror ties, but perhaps it was some black ops type thing he wasn't supposed to talk about.

The type of thing she'd seen only in movies.

Yet he'd told her.

She certainly knew better than to go to a hotel room with a strange man she'd barely just met, but at the moment, what choice did she have? She couldn't go back to her flat. Shouldn't call any of her friends on her mobile.

Not without risking harm coming to them.

Emma knew next-to-nothing about Hunter, yet if her choice was him or those two men she'd run from?

Her gut told her she could trust him.

She brushed the tears away as he stepped closer, feeling foolish. She wasn't even certain if they were tears of laughter or sheer exhaustion at this point. His gaze briefly dropped to her chest, and as her eyes followed his, she blushed, realizing the lacy outline of her bra was now evident through her thin cashmere sweater.

She hadn't exactly been planning to run through a

downpour and go back to the hotel with a strange man. She sniffed again, looking away.

"Don't cry," he said gruffly.

"I'm not," she said, swiping at her eyes again. Feeling the wetness of her tears on the back of her hand. "I'm perfectly fine. What floor is your room on, anyway?"

The corner of his mouth quirked up. "You're not crying?"

"Of course not—don't be ridiculous."

"Eight."

"Eight?"

"The floor."

"Oh. Right."

She avoided his gaze, glancing at the advert for London restaurants on one wall of the elevator. The slightly worn edges of the carpet.

"I guess the saying about Brits is true," he commented dryly.

"And what saying is that?" she asked, regaining some of her composure as the elevator dinged at his floor and the doors opened.

"You have a stiff upper lip."

She huffed, trying to hide her amusement as she stepped off into the hallway. "And are all American men as rude as you?"

"I'm pretty sure I've been nothing but a gentleman, princess," he said, easily falling in step beside her. Fortunately, she'd chosen the right direction to walk in. Or else he was just humoring her.

He took a quick glance over his shoulder behind them, then rested one large hand on the small of her back. They could've been any other couple walking to their hotel room—except she was drenched. Frightened. Exhausted.

"Not hardly," she said. "You just pointed out that I was standing in the elevator crying—there's hardly anything gentleman-like about that."

"And I was supposed to just ignore a woman crying and stand there like some asshole? That doesn't seem very chivalrous. Not that I'm usually the chivalrous sort—you must bring it out in me."

"I'm beginning to think your tough-guy act is just a show."

He raised his eyebrows.

"The tattoos, the scowl on your face."

"Flattery will get you nowhere," he muttered, pulling a card from one of the pockets of his cargo pants. He swiped the keycard to the door of his room and shoved it open, taking one last glance around the hallway. "Home sweet—well, whatever the hell it is. You know, usually when I bring a woman back to my hotel room, I'm trying to undress her, not offer her dry clothes."

"How comforting," she murmured, taking in the piles of rumpled clothes, his military issue duffel bag, and backpack scattered on the floor.

He secured the door, taking a cursory glance into the bathroom, and then swaggered by her—really, there was no other description for the way he moved. His broad shoulders framed the bulging biceps of his arms, the muscles of his back. His hips narrowed where his pants perfectly hung, showcasing his ass. Why yes, she was actually staring at this man's ass.

Did her rescuer have to be so bloody good-looking?

Hunter crouched down, digging around in his

duffel bag. Grumbling to himself, he stood, tossing both the backpack and duffel bag onto his neatly made bed, pulling the earpiece from his ear as he muttered a curse.

A loud noise in the hall startled her, and she jumped, her heart racing.

"Ice machine. Damn thing makes noise day and night."

Her eyes widened as he pulled a gun from his bag, checking the cartridge before setting it on the night table. "I've got a gun and a K-Bar," he said, his blue eyes meeting hers.

"K-Bar?"

"Military-issued knife. I don't want you to be frightened, but we don't know who's been following you. If they tried to grab you in Kabul and ransacked your apartment, we'll need a hell of a lot more firepower than this."

"Firepower?"

"It's not like I'm carrying around a couple HK416 assault rifles. We need to be careful."

"Maybe I should just go back to the police."

"Maybe so. But if someone is following you in the meantime, I want to be prepared. My goal was to get you out of the damn pub unharmed. Turning over the information you have is second on my list of priorities."

He stood and stripped his wet tee-shirt above his head, revealing an abdomen full of rippling muscles. She forced herself to look away, to look around the hotel room, to let her gaze rest anywhere but on him.

His low chuckle sent a feeling of warmth through her shivering body, and she could feel the blush spreading across her cheeks.

"Hell, I don't mind if you watch." He winked as she hastened a glance back, much to her utter mortification. There was a third tattoo—some sort of round, tribal symbol across his broad pec. Briefly, she wondered what other tattoos he had—maybe something across his back. Something underneath his cargos. No doubt he'd gladly show her if she asked—and there was absolutely zero chance of that happening.

"Let me grab some clothes for you. I'd offer you a warm shower, but we can't stay here. Not at the risk someone else was watching us. Let's gather up some things and go."

He pulled a clean tee-shirt from his pile of things and tossed it toward her.

She caught it clumsily and then glanced around.

"Go change in the bathroom if you want. Me? I'm not shy." He unbuttoned his wet cargo pants and pushed them down, and then she was turning, moving toward the bathroom. But not before she'd seen those tight, black boxer briefs—the thick muscles on his thighs. The very large, ah, package concealed beneath his boxers.

Good heavens.

Pink tinged her cheeks as she stared at her reflection in the bathroom, and yes—you could see the lace of her bra though the wet, light pink cashmere sweater. The outline of her nipples as they pebbled in the cold. Silly her for wearing a sexy lace bra while outrunning the bad guys.

Hmmph.

She had a whole drawerful of beautiful lingerie they'd probably torn through back at her flat. She'd have to burn it all now. She couldn't imagine wearing or wanting any of her things after grubby hands had sifted through her intimate belongings.

She dropped her backpack onto the counter, eyeing the water stains disdainfully, and quickly pulled off her soggy sweater. Tugged on the oversized tee-shirt of Hunter's—and bloody hell, it even smelled like him.

Clean. A hint of spice.

Hadn't he been deployed somewhere on a mission?

How'd his clothes smell so damn good?

She inhaled, suddenly feeling foolish. Never mind that his tee-shirt was now resting against her lace-clad breasts, covering her skin. The cotton had touched him—and there was something sexy as hell about wearing a man's shirt.

About Hunter's need to protect her.

She was being ridiculous though. They needed to get out of here, not wait around while she swooned over what was likely an insignificant act. She was soaking wet. They were on the run. And they needed to get the documents turned over to the proper authorities.

Opening her backpack, she pulled out her mobile. She had three new messages from friends, but she hastily texted her neighbor.

*Someone's been following me. If you see anything else suspicious around my flat, ring the police immediately.*

She glanced toward the bathroom door, which she'd left ajar, and heard Hunter zipping up a bag. Deciding she had a minute to spare while Hunter gathered up the rest of his things, she turned on the hair dryer and quickly dried her dampened locks. She'd just about kill for a hot bath at the moment, but not feeling like a drowned rat would be a start.

"All set, princess?" a deep voice asked, sending her shrieking.

One large hand caught hers while the other neatly nabbed the hairdryer from midair. "It's just me," Hunter said, letting his fingers curl around her own. Holding her hand for a beat while she trembled.

"Holy shit," she protested, tugging her hand away. Immediately regretting the loss of his touch. "Do you always sneak up on people like that?"

"You knew I was right in the other room—and besides, you left the door partway open."

Emma blew out an exasperated breath. "That's because I wanted to be aware if anyone was coming! You know, in case they tried to break down the door of the hotel room and come in here after us?"

He quirked a brow. "So you turned on the hair dryer? Where exactly were you planning to run in the bathroom anyway? It's not like you can stand there and stop them with a blast of hot air."

"No—I just—never mind. I was soaking wet."

"Gotcha, princess." He eyed her, his blue eyes warming. "You look pretty good in my shirt. Too damn good. Anyway, let's roll out."

Sighing, she stuffed her wet sweater into the plastic bag meant for laundry and then put it into her backpack. "And where exactly are we 'rolling'? Perhaps you should just escort me to the police station. They didn't believe me before, but after that little incident at the pub? Maybe I can drop off the papers and go. I'm sure it's already all over the evening news."

"Uh-huh. And what's to stop those guys from coming after you? Doesn't matter if you deliver the goods. You've seen it. Read whatever papers they want back."

A chill snaked down her spine.

She had read it. Had a backup copy.

Even if she handed off everything tonight—they'd still want her.

This wouldn't end until they'd found her.

"I contacted my CO. As soon as you fill me in on whatever papers you have in your hot little hands, we can help you. Take them through the proper military channels. Turn them over to the Brits—guessing MI6 if you're somehow mixed up with this terrorist group."

"You think?" she commented dryly. "Too bad the police officer I spoke with earlier couldn't have cared less."

"Let's go," he said, a large hand closing over her shoulder. "Stay behind me," he added, pausing at the door. "Normally I'd say, 'ladies first,' but with these assholes after you? Not a chance in hell."

"Such a gentleman," she murmured.

His hand rested at his waist as he peered through the peephole of the door, and she realized his gun was there. No telling where he'd hidden his knife.

Hunter probably was used to charging into situations guns blazing. She'd seen SEALs in movies—all decked out in their military gear. No fear as they stormed into the unknown. Is that was this guy did every day?

It was a far cry from her life.

His blue eyes blazed as he glanced back at her. "Far from it."

"Excuse me?" she asked, bewildered.

"I'm far from being a gentleman. But I'll protect

you—and that's all that matters right now."

# Chapter 4

Hunter pulled open the door of his hotel room, feeling Emma's small frame trembling behind him. He shifted his backpack to one shoulder and stepped into the carpeted hall. It sucked to leave the rest of his things behind, but this was no time to gather up all his belongings. Maybe he'd be back—maybe not.

At the moment, he just needed to get Emma out of here unharmed.

Fucking hell.

How someone like her had gotten mixed up in this defied explanation. She was a British archeologist—an academic. She wrote papers and did research for a living. He jumped out of airplanes and infiltrated terrorist camps. Fought the bad guys. Deployed all over the goddamn world.

But a woman like her?

This situation was FUBAR—and he needed to get her the hell out of it. Sure, he could drop her off at the nearest police station and be on his merry way. Hop on a flight back to the States, assuming those two assholes in the pub were taken care of.

But to leave her here alone? Unarmed and frightened?

There wasn't a chance in hell of that happening.

His gaze swept the vacant hall. Every door was closed, but that didn't mean there were no threats. Despite his precautions, someone could have followed them up here. Could be casing the place now.

Which was why they needed to leave as quickly as possible.

His phone buzzed with a new text from Mason.

*Finishing up with the Brits. Flight's leaving out of Heathrow at 0800.*

Shit.

He quickly thumbed a response.

*They take you down to the station?*

Mason's reply flashed on his screen.

*Yep. Had to call the CO and American Embassy. Headed back soon.*

Hunter clenched his jaw. He should be glad they were on their way home—neatly extricating themselves from a situation they shouldn't have been involved with in the first place.

But as for Emma?

He'd bring her back to Little Creek with him if he had to.

He'd sure as hell feel a lot better on familiar territory—with his SEAL team close by. He could get whatever documents she had to the proper British authorities, but leaving her behind? No fucking way. Not when there were still men looking for her.

"I don't suppose you have some quiet little house in the country we could hide out in," he said over his shoulder as they walked down the hall.

"A quiet house in the country?" she laughed. "Why, are you looking to extend your vacation?"

He muttered a curse. Yeah, that was just his thing—a bed and breakfast that served scones and clotted cream every morning. In her dreams. "My CO has us on a flight tomorrow out of Heathrow. And I'm not leaving you alone here, princess."

"London's a big city. I can find somewhere to stay aside from my flat. If you're returning home, you needn't concern yourself with me."

"Too late for that," he muttered, feeling his gut clench. Uneasiness rolled over him at the thought of leaving her alone. He glanced back, not missing the fear and concern etched across her face. The uneasiness in her green eyes. "We just need somewhere to spend the night, and then I'll bring you with me."

"Bring me where? Back to the U.S.? In case you're forgetting, I just got back to London. I can't go running off again. I have my work. My family and friends."

He paused and nailed her with a glare. "And where exactly are you planning on going? You already told me your apartment's been ransacked. That you don't want to drag your friends into this."

"Agreed—my flat isn't safe right now."

"Flat, apartment—whatever the hell you want to call it. You can't go back there. Not now—not ever."

He turned and continued walking toward the stairwell.

"What do you mean I can't go back there 'ever'?"

she asked, sounding more irritated than frightened. "And why are we walking this way? The elevator's back there."

"We're taking the stairs. Just a precaution. And as I was saying, I'll arrange to bring you back with me."

"Back? Back where?"

"I'm stationed in Little Creek. It's near Virginia Beach—about four hours south of DC, depending on traffic, of course."

"I can't go back with you," she said.

"And I can't leave you here. Your research—you can do that anywhere, right? All you need is your laptop. I'm a Navy SEAL supposedly on R&R—I have to get back to base at some point. But I'll feel better with you nearby until this entire shit show is over."

"I'm not your responsibility. You certainly don't need to feel obligated to offer me some sort of protection."

The elevator dinged behind them, and he glanced back, watching a middle-aged couple get off. Walk in the other direction.

Emma stopped behind him as he paused at the door to the stairwell, listening. The small square window didn't show much—anyone could be crouching down behind it. Waiting on the level below.

Emma's floral scent filled the air as she edged closer behind him, and his groin tightened. Yeah, like now was the appropriate time to be thinking with his dick. He'd already had her in his hotel room and hadn't even touched her. He was here to protect her—that was all.

The fact that she had his libido rising was

inconvenient, but this wasn't some chick he'd bang and then walk away from. Never see again. He'd felt protective toward her since the moment she'd bumped into him earlier—all green eyes, pale skin, and gorgeous hair. And when he'd realized she was the one those assholes had been after?

He'd seen red. The idea of letting her out of his sight now was unfathomable.

"Why are we stopping?" she asked as she tried to peer around his shoulder. "Is someone there?"

Fucking hell.

She was so small, the top of her head barely reached his shoulders. Her lips were at his bicep as she tried to peer around him—and he could feel her breath on his skin. Wouldn't he love to be able to turn and pull her against him. Back her against the door. Kiss her until she whimpered and gasped for more.

He was hard everywhere she was soft, and yeah. It would be pretty damn spectacular.

Like they had time for that right now.

"Just listening," he said, his voice gravel. "Making sure no one is hiding in the stairwell. I doubt anyone followed us up here, but I'm not taking any chances."

He didn't miss the intake of her breath. The way she stiffened behind him.

"Oh, right. Of course."

Hell. He didn't want to frighten her any more than she already was. He should keep his damn mouth shut. But was it better to keep her in the dark? She was clueless about the most basic of precautions. He clenched his fist, moving his hand back to his weapon.

Hunter was just pushing open the door to the

stairwell when they were startled by angry shouts behind them. By the screams of the couple walking the other way.

Two men came charging off the elevator, looking left and right. Emma shrieked behind him as they came running down the hall, and Hunter tugged her in front of him as he grabbed his firearm. Pushed her through the doorway of the stairwell.

"Run!" he commanded. "Don't wait for me."

She didn't question him or look back, just dashed down the stairs, red hair flying behind her. Hunter muttered under his breath and ducked out of the way as shots ran down the corridor. As the heavy door shut behind him. Grabbing a wet umbrella someone had left on the stairs, he jammed it into the door handle.

Yeah. That would stop them for all of five seconds.

Fucking hell.

"Oh my God!" Emma exclaimed breathlessly as they raced down the flights. "They came after us! They're right up there. Ohmigod ohmigod!"

Hunter glanced up, watching as the door rattled.

Four-three-two—Boom!

Kicked open in no time.

He grabbed Emma and pulled her into the hall on the fourth floor. Didn't look back as they ran. It looked exactly like the floor they'd just left. Carpeted hallway. Closed doors. But it was better to run to another part of the building before the men began shooting at them from above in the stairwell.

"Holy crap!" Emma said as they ran down the hall. "Who were those guys?"

"Friends of the ones from the pub. They probably

all tie back to the terrorist group after you. There's another stairwell this way," he said, hustling her along. His arm went around her waist, his hand securely gripping her hip. Guiding her in front of him.

"Are you sure?"

"I memorized the floorplan of the hotel when I checked in."

Hunter didn't bother checking this stairwell, just pushed the door open, tugging Emma alongside him. Keeping his arm snared around her slender waist. If someone came from behind, he could shield her with his body. Protect her.

But when they were out in the open?

He needed to move her somewhere safe.

"They're probably going down to the lobby. The other stairs are near the front of the hotel, but we should be able to go out the side. Hell. I hope Mason doesn't run into those assholes on his way back."

"I hear sirens," Emma said. "The police are already on their way. Oh my God—all those poor people hiding in their rooms. They must be scared out of their minds!"

"No doubt someone called the police after hearing the gunshots. They'll probably lock down the building when they arrive. But we don't know how many of those guys are here coming after you, which is why we're leaving."

"This is bloody unbelievable," she muttered, hustling along in front of him. "My entire life is turning into some sort of action movie—and I hate action movies."

Hunter smirked, watching her red hair swish back and forth as she ran down the stairs. This was not time to be ogling Emma, but hell.

She was gorgeous no matter what she was doing.

They ran down the stairs to the first floor, Hunter pausing at the door that opened to the lobby. Ten feet away was an exit to a side street. They just had to cross a small part of the lobby and get through the door. Ten feet until they were out.

"We can wait for the police," Emma said breathlessly. "Turn over the information."

"We can. They'll be here shortly—"

A door to the stairwell above them suddenly burst open, banging loudly against the wall, and footsteps pounded down the stairs. Hunter grabbed Emma and pushed open the door as a man came running down the stairs from several floors above. The concierge was ducking behind his desk as hotel security rushed about the lobby with walkie-talkies, and the man behind the check-in counter was talking rapidly on the phone, nervously eyeing the front door.

Hunter didn't speak with any of them, just pushed Emma through the door to the side street. Glanced around.

Sirens sounded in the distance, but he wasn't waiting for backup.

"Where are we going?" she asked.

"Don't know. Don't care." Hunter hustled her over to a parked car, dropping his backpack to the ground and grabbing his tools.

"Are you going to steal a car?" she asked incredulously as he quickly picked the lock.

"Borrow. I'm borrowing a car. Go around and climb in," he said, ducking down to hotwire the engine. It purred to life as Emma sank into the passenger seat, and a moment later he was pulling out into traffic, watching in the rearview mirror as a man came bursting out the side door of the hotel. He clenched the steering wheel, watching as the man looked both ways, searching for them.

As much as he'd love to peel out of there, the God-awful traffic in London prohibited it. And there was no point in drawing attention to themselves when they'd left unnoticed. Were hiding in plain sight. Someone would certainly notice their car missing, but those assholes after Emma were momentarily without a clue.

He signaled and made a right turn, cursing under his breath. Trying to get used to driving on the wrong side of the car. The wrong side of the road.

Fucking hell.

He could fly a helicopter. Drive a goddamn tank if he needed to. But this ridiculousness of putting the driver on the right side of the car was unnerving.

And wasn't that an understatement.

Emma released a breath, shrinking down into the seat beside him. Closing her eyes as she exhaled. She clutched her backpack tightly, her fingers turning white.

"Breathe," he commanded. "We're safe. We'll find somewhere to hide out while I figure out our next move."

"I know. I know—it's just. I can't believe this is happening. Any of it. A week ago, I was doing research for my paper—pretending to be an aid worker, perhaps, but nothing terribly uncouth. Just another foreigner visiting Kabul. And now I have international terrorists chasing after me."

"I think we should head out of the city," he said, his voice low. "I don't know how many of those guys there are, but we need to lay low. I'll copy whatever papers you have and get them to my CO. He can deal directly with the rest of the Brits. Share them with the Pentagon."

"Right. I already made copies on my thumb drive. I have the hard copies, too, but we can upload them easily to a computer and send them off."

Has gaze swept to her. "Where's the thumb drive?"

She swallowed nervously.

"Emma, I think we've already established that you can trust me."

"It's sewn into the lining of my backpack. I have my laptop as well, but I wiped it from there, just to be safe. In case it was stolen. Luckily I kept it on my person as my flat was ransacked—all my research is there. I keep backups of course, but bloody hell. I don't need to lose all of my work as well in the midst of this disaster."

Hunter let out a low whistle. "Mind telling me what's on the papers you found? I've been shot at, chased out of a hotel, run out of a pub—I think at this point you can assume I'm on your side. Never mind the fact that the whole reason I was in the damn pub conducting surveillance in the first place is because I was looking for you."

"Looking for me? What on Earth do you mean?"

"Our latest SITREP indicated there was a missing British archeologist in Afghanistan. It seems that a friend of yours went to the American Embassy when you disappeared. They contacted the Brits, and the rest, as they say, is history. Mason and I happened to be in the right place at the right time and did a little off-the-books work."

"Lily. I left my friend Lily in the market a week

ago. I spotted some men I thought were looking for me, which is why I deserted her there. I didn't want her involved in any of this. I'm sure she was worried sick when I never went back to the housing the aid workers were staying in, but I didn't have any choice. It was safest to just leave immediately—disassociate myself with all of them."

"You haven't tried to contact her?" Hunter asked, glancing sideways at her. Watching as she nervously bit her lip, her eyes worriedly meeting his.

"No. I feel terrible, but I had to get out of Kabul as quickly as possible. And I didn't want her to be involved in any of this. I took those papers I discovered, but she didn't know anything about it. No one did."

"Mind telling me how you snuck back into Britain?"

She blew out a sigh. "It's kind of a long, complicated story."

"I figured. Enough about that though. Tell me what's in the documents you have."

She nodded. Searched his gaze before he glanced back at the road. "It's a list of targets—terror targets. Sites in the U.S. and Europe. The entire document was pages and pages long—but I grabbed the list from the pile of materials so they wouldn't notice that the entire thing was missing right away. I wish I had time to copy all of it—photograph it with my phone or something, but I stumbled upon it so quickly I just grabbed what I could without thinking. I thought I'd be helping—I didn't really think of the consequences. That they'd come after me if they discovered who took them."

"Where'd you find it?" he asked incredulously.

"Outside of Kabul. I wanted to visit some of the areas I've been researching once more. I stumbled upon a parcel that must've been inadvertently dropped. It certainly wasn't very well hidden. Some of the papers were coming out, so I looked at it."

"And took what you could."

"Unfortunately, yes. As soon as I realized what I'd found, I decided to leave Kabul as quickly as possible. I was there on a 6-month work visa but made plans to leave the following day."

"Did you tell anyone?"

"Not a soul. I left my closest friend Lily alone in the market—I literally just turned and headed off in a different direction when I became concerned. I told my friend I'd meet her in ten minutes, but I had no plans to go back. I just left."

"And they saw you," he ascertained, narrowing his gaze as he followed the signs leaving downtown London. The city was beginning to light up for the night, and his eyes swept over to the Tower Bridge. Damn shame he hadn't gotten to really play tourist while he was here, but that was life.

Duty called.

"Apparently so," she said. "A colleague of mine told me that some men were asking about me the day before. I thought visiting the bazaar would be a good move—get me out of there." She blew out a breath, rubbing her shoulders with one slender hand as she relaxed into the seat.

"You're tired."

"Yeah. It's been a long few days—a long week. I want to hand over the information to whoever needs to see it—extricate myself from this entirely."

"I'm not sure that's possible," he said, frowning.

"Get some sleep. I'll find somewhere to go for the night."

"But what are you going to do? Your flight leaves in the morning."

"I'll catch a different flight. As soon as we find a safe place to stay, I'll contact my CO. Let him know the change of plans."

She yawned, and he narrowed his gaze. "Sleep, Emma. You're safe with me."

"You don't even know where you're going," she protested. "I'm the local here. I should probably be the one driving. Have you ever even driven on the right side of the road before?"

"Not a chance in hell are you driving—you'll fall asleep at the wheel. And what do you think I'm doing right now? Driving on the damn wrong side of the road. Besides, that's what GPS and road signs are for. I'm pretty sure I'm capable of finding a place to stay for the night."

"Typical man who thinks he knows everything," she murmured, closing her eyes.

Hunter quirked a brow. "What makes you think I'm typical?"

"Touché," she said softly.

A moment later, she was fast asleep. Her chest gently rose and fell, her lips parted slightly, and Hunter felt a tug in his chest he didn't want to examine too closely. He muttered a curse. Usually if he spent this much time with a woman it was in bed. Or they were at least naked, he thought with a smirk. Bed, sofa, kitchen table—he wasn't picky. Usually he was trying to undress a woman, not offer her dry clothes.

Hunter grabbed his phone from the center

console, pushing the button for speaker as he called Mason.

"The hotel is goddamn mob-scene," Mason said as he answered. "What the hell happened?"

"They tracked us to my hotel room," Hunter said, eyeing Emma. She remained sound asleep, and he relaxed slightly. Hell. Since when did he concern himself with not waking a sleeping woman?

Since he'd run into her.

Since he'd discovered that goddamn terrorists were after her.

Her head was resting against the window, her long red hair tumbling down over her shoulders as she quietly slept. His tee-shirt was massive on her, drowning her feminine figure, but there was something damn appealing about seeing her in his clothes. He'd just met the women a few hours ago. There was no reason he should feel possessive toward her—but there it was.

He'd protected her. Made sure she felt safe.

His chest filled with masculine pride—the only better feeling might be if she was beneath him. In his arms and in his bed. Her thighs parting to welcome his now aching cock.

But a night like that wasn't happening.

Where the hell they were going he didn't have a clue. But all that mattered was keeping her safe.

"Left a few bullet holes in the place," Mason said. "I couldn't even get down the hall to my room."

"Where are you?"

"Down in the lobby. The place is crawling with police. Never mind that I just left the station—now they have a shit ton of other questions. Gonna have to call the CO again."

"We shouldn't have been involved in the first place."

"Nope. Too late for that now though. You know what they say—better to beg for forgiveness than to ask permission."

Hunter guffawed. "Who the hell says that?"

"People. People do. So where are you anyway? I assume since you're calling you're not still being chased."

"Not at the moment," Hunter grunted, eyeing the rearview mirror. "Emma's got some info we need to pass on though. We'll find somewhere safe to stay for the night and I'll send the documents she discovered."

"You need any help?"

"The situation is under control."

"Roger that. And how does Emma feel about spending the night with you? She didn't seem too thrilled with you at the pub."

"What can I say? Rescue a woman from the bad guys a few times and they change their tune."

Mason chuffed out a laugh. "Right. I'm sure she's crawling all over you—not. Better make sure you get a room with two beds—she sure the hell wasn't looking at you with interest earlier. Will you be on the flight out in the morning?"

"Unlikely. I want to lay low for the while. Make sure she's safe. And don't worry about our sleeping arrangements," he muttered, irritation rising in him. Where Emma slept was nobody's business but his own. He sure the hell didn't want Mason imagining her naked body beneath the sheets.

"Bring her back to Little Creek with you. It's safe there with half the damn Navy around. Hell, we've got our team, Ice's team—we'll watch out for her."

"I damn well might. Better than letting these assholes chase her all over London. Even if she turned over the papers she has, they've seen her. They know where she lives. What she looks like. It's not safe for her to stay here alone."

"Agreed. Let me know if you need backup. I can head out and meet you wherever the hell you're going."

"Will do."

Hunter heard commotion through the phone as Mason muttered a curse. "Maybe I should just head to a pub and find another woman to spend the night with. What the hell—finish off our little UK stop in style. Doesn't look like I'll get back to my room anytime soon. And you're off playing hero to the woman you rescued."

"Yeah, just how I prefer to spend my nights," Hunter muttered. "Outrunning men shooting at me."

"You made a hell of an impression here," Mason quipped.

"Not the kind I wanted. Over and out," Hunter said.

He gripped the steering wheel after they'd said their goodbyes, glancing at the road signs. Stealing a glance over at Emma, sleeping soundly beside him.

Hell.

What exactly had this woman gotten herself mixed up in?

## Chapter 5

Emma awoke with a start as a car door closed, looking around in confusion in the dark. She blinked and sat up straighter, rubbing her stiff neck as her eyes adjusted to the darkness. Her mouth felt like it had been stuffed with cotton, and her stomach rumbled in hunger. How many hours had passed since they'd left London?

She shifted in her seat, her feet bumping into her backpack. Her eyes followed the movement outside, and she watched as Hunter crossed in front of the bonnet of the car, his profile showing in the lights from a cottage he'd stopped at.

Unwelcome memories of the past few hours came quickly flooding back.

Running down the stairs in the hotel.

Stealing a car.

Falling asleep as the American Navy SEAL she'd met hurriedly drove them out of London.

She glanced down at the oversized shirt she had on, remembering her own soggy sweater stashed in her backpack, and let out a sigh as she leaned back against the seat once more.

Hunter pulled open the door to her side of the car, the interior dome illuminating his muscled forearm. His thick fingers wrapped around hers as he helped her stand, and he reached in and grabbed her backpack, clutching it in his large hand.

His spicy, clean scent washed over her, and she resisted the urge to lean closer. To let his strength and warmth surround her.

She didn't even know this man, yet she felt safe with him. Which was utterly ridiculous because he was one man against an entire group that appeared to be chasing after her. If they wanted her badly enough, they'd find a way. He'd be powerless to stop them, and she'd be powerless to avoid being kidnapped. She didn't need to get out of London, she needed to get out of the damn country.

"How long was I asleep?" she asked as he released her hand.

"A couple of hours," he said, quietly shutting the door. He looked down, meeting her gaze. Somehow he looked even more dangerous in the dark—the scruff of his beard. His chiseled features. The broad muscles across his torso and arms. His muscled chest filled out his tee-shirt in a way that was positively drool-worthy. And for some reason this man had assumed the role of her protector. That was fine for the evening, but what exactly was she supposed to do the next day? The next week?

Literally her entire life was in shambles.

"Are you okay?" he asked.

"Fine," she said, brushing some of her hair back from her face. His eyes followed her movements, and she felt herself inexplicably feeling calmer as he watched her. He was attentive and aware. Concerned. Maybe she was nothing more than his latest mission, but at the moment, she could use any and all help she could get.

"Nothing like sightseeing in Europe while on the run from a terrorist cell," he muttered. "This must be the worst R&R in history."

Her stomach dropped.

Of course he'd be resentful that he'd gotten mixed up in this mess. He'd already said he was on his way back from some sort of operation. That he was just meant to be listening in on a conversation. She didn't know much about SEALs, but she knew the military deployed all over the world. Same as the British forces. He was probably tired and ready for a vacation of sorts, and now he was stuck here babysitting her.

"Where are we?" she asked, gazing around the small lot. The small cottage. There were two other cars, but the place was otherwise deserted.

"Bed and breakfast. Not exactly my thing, but if anyone asks, we're together. There's just one bed in the room I got us, but don't worry, I can crash on the floor. I've slept in a hell of a lot of worse places than this."

"Wonderful," she murmured. "I always hoped to have a brash, bossy, pretend American boyfriend."

"Beggars can't be choosers, princess. Would you rather I left you alone in the pub back in London?"

"Bloody hell, of course not," she said, walking across the gravel lot toward the building.

"Aren't you in a good mood."

"I'm exhausted. I'm scared. And you've just pointed out that you were supposed to be here on a holiday, not running around with the likes of me."

"A holiday," he muttered. "Of course you're my priority now," he said with a scowl. "You were my responsibility the second you walked into that pub. I certainly would have preferred that we met under different circumstances, but there it is. I'm not going to complain about helping a beautiful woman. Let's go to our room and send those files. Get the rest of the military in on this. I don't think anyone followed us here, because I drove around in circles for over an hour. I'll have to ditch the car once I get you safely inside. We passed some large fields with clusters of trees in the countryside. I'll leave it there and hike back."

"Right now?"

"Can't have it here in the morning. The owner has likely filed a police report. Which means we'll have to find a new ride back to London to catch our flight."

"So we're stranded here."

"Momentarily. We'll get a ride back. Hell, Mason can come pick us up if need be, but he's supposed to be flying out in the morning. And I don't want anyone following him here to us. That kind of defeats the purpose of leaving the city."

"What about your flight?"

"I'm changing it. And taking you with me."

"How lovely. Do you usually go around stealing cars back in the States?"

"No, this is my first grand larceny," he quipped.

She looked at him in disbelief as he winked at her and then produced a key from the pocket of his pants as they made their way to the room. Hunter slid the key into the lock and pushed open the door, and she wanted to cringe at the sight—wrought-iron bed, handmade quilts, framed needlepoint on the walls. It was about as old-fashioned and unromantic as one could imagine. Not that she and Hunter were here on some sort of romantic getaway—far from it. But why anyone would think that stealing their lover away to a bed and breakfast for a romantic weekend was a wonderful notion, she hadn't a clue.

"Looks like it could've been decorated by my grandma," Hunter muttered, setting both backpacks on the bed.

"It's a far cry from my flat in London. Of course, my flat was apparently torn apart, so this will have to do."

She dug through her backpack, pulling out her mobile. Her heart dropped as she saw a text from her neighbor.

*The police are back. Some strange guy was here looking for you.*

"Bloody hell," she said.

Hunter's blue gaze shifted to her. "What's wrong?"

"Someone was looking for me at my flat earlier."

"What time?"

"The text from my neighbor says 2100. What's so funny?" she asked as she saw Hunter's lips quirk.

"Nothing—I just always forget that Brits use military time. Civilians never understand me back home."

"How lovely. I guess you missed the part that some strange man was looking for me back at my flat. That's twice in one day that I know of."

"Nope, didn't miss that at all, princess," he said, walking over and taking her phone. "Has this thing been on?"

"No, actually I turned it off earlier. What are you doing?"

He pulled the back of her phone cover off and popped out the SIM card, then dropped it to the ground and smashed it with his foot.

"Hey!" she exclaimed, irritation rising through her.

"If they could find your home, they can track you on your phone. Do you have any other electronic devices?"

"My laptop is in my backpack—I thought I already mentioned that."

"Don't turn it on either. We'll use mine to send the documents."

Hunter sank onto the bed, rummaging around in his own backpack. He pulled a small laptop out and turned it on, entering in a string of numbers. "Let me see the thumb drive you have. We'll upload the files right now."

"I need your knife."

He raised his eyebrows.

"I sewed it into the lining of my backpack—I don't want to ruin the entire thing to get it back out. I'm just going to slice the seam."

He pulled up a pants leg and pulled out an incredibly sharp knife. She took it from him in disbelief and carefully sliced open a few inches of the lining, retrieving the thumb drive. "This has what you need. I almost wish I'd never taken them in the first place."

"Almost?" he asked, sticking the device into a port on his computer and rapidly firing off an email.

"Well, if it stops a terror attack, then it was worth all the trouble. I'm not sure that my own life is safe anymore, but good heavens. I don't think so highly of myself that I'd put my own safety above that of others. Hundreds of people were injured and many killed during the bombings in London on 7/7. On 9/11, there were thousands killed in the U.S."

"That's what solidified my career in the Navy."

"And many others, I'd imagine. In the U.K., as well. It certainly changed the world, didn't it?"

"All set," he said, pulling the thumb drive out of the port. "You want to hold onto this?"

"It's all yours. Give it to your military or turn it over to the authorities here if you prefer. I'm done carrying it around."

Hunter turned the small thumb drive over in his hand then slid it into the pocket of his cargo pants. "I'll keep it on my person. I need to get rid of the car though. Will you be okay here? I'll come back as quickly as possible. I made sure we weren't followed."

"I'll be fine," she assured him. "If anyone comes in, I'll just scream for help."

He raised his eyebrows.

"Well, you've destroyed my phone."

"Wasn't safe, princess."

She blew out a breath. "I know. Just go—ditch the car or do whatever you need to do. Set it up in flames for all I care. I'm exhausted."

Hunter rose and crossed the room to the door. "I'll be back soon. Don't open the door for anyone."

"Of course. It's not like I'd think you'd go to all this trouble to rescue me then abandon me at a bed and breakfast."

His lips quirked up. "I'm sure it's been done before—this place could scare off many a guy."

She laughed despite herself. "I'd say that it would

take more than a little needlepoint to keep you away. You've already assured me that you're not a typical man."

"Far from it," he said gruffly. His gaze met hers briefly, and a moment later, he was gone.

\*\*\*

Hunter walked back into the room an hour later, pocketing the key, not surprised to see that Emma had fallen asleep on the bed. She'd looked exhausted earlier, with dark circles under her eyes, highlighted even more due to her fair skin.

It had been all he could do not to pull her close for a moment. Promise he'd keep her safe. She'd been through a hell of a lot more than most civilians and was holding up better than he'd expected. Aside from the tears in the elevator earlier, she'd been calm and collected ever since.

No telling how she'd be feeling tomorrow once reality set in. It was unsettling to have someone break into your home, to go through all of your belongings, and to know that she'd been followed? Chased? Shot at?

He shook his head.

Emma was beneath the quilt on the bed, the bulkiness of it covering her slender frame, her red hair fanned out around her. The other pillow was untouched beside her, looking absolutely inviting. Wouldn't he fucking love to climb in bed beside her and pull her body close to his, but he wasn't about to sneak up on a sleeping woman.

He wasn't a saint, but even he had boundaries he wouldn't cross. Not that he expected an engraved invitation, but a woman certainly had to be awake before he'd make the first move. And this was hardly the appropriate time to be trying moves of any sort.

He grabbed an extra blanket and the pillow, tossing them onto an armchair in the corner. As soon as he was done in the bathroom, he was crashing as well. There was no telling what they'd need to do tomorrow, and he wanted to be ready and alert first thing.

Same as always when he was on an op.

He turned and strode into the bathroom, doing a double-take. Emma's cashmere sweater was lying across a fluffy white towel on the claw foot bath tub, but that wasn't what had him coming to a halt. What made his groin tighten.

The palest pink lace bra hung from a fancy hook on the back of the door, along with a skimpy pair of lacy thong panties.

Knowing he shouldn't, he reached out and touched the lace cup of her bra.

Groaned.

The entire bathroom smelled of the rose-scented soap the bed and breakfast had provided, and he saw drops of water in the bathtub. She'd bathed there, the water and soap sliding over her bare skin. No doubt he would've been happy to assist, had he been around, but he had a feeling she'd have politely declined.

Hell.

If she'd left some of her clothes in here, that meant she was asleep in his tee-shirt. Naked.

He'd take a quick shower himself before he crashed for the night and tried to ignore the beautiful woman sleeping mere feet away.

Grumbling at the flimsy shower curtain he had to pull all the way around the old-fashioned tub, he grabbed the handheld sprayer and lifted it above his head. The entire set-up wasn't exactly suited to a man who was 6'2," but at least it was a shower.

He toweled off, heading back into the room wearing only his boxer briefs. No sense in freaking Emma out if she awoke to find him sleeping buck naked. Nothing like a little morning wood to scare off a woman who barely knew him.

He pulled his cell phone from the pocket of his discarded cargo pants, seeing the latest message from his CO.

*Change of plans. You leave in 48 hours. Flight's on Wed at 2300.*

Damn it. What the hell was he supposed to do for two days with Emma?

He quickly thumbed a response.

*You get the intel I sent?*

His CO's reply came immediately.

*Affirmative. Already shared it with the Brits and the Pentagon. Lie low for a few days until some of these guys are rounded up.*

Hunter clenched his fist, grabbing his adapter and charger from his backpack. Lie low? He was a goddamn Navy SEAL. He was used to being in the center of the action, deploying on ops, focusing on his training. He certainly wasn't used to hiding out with a woman for a couple of days while he let others handle the situation.

He crossed the room, irritated, and grabbed his pillow and blanket, tossing them onto the floor. His blood boiled as he stared up at the ceiling, his thoughts on everything that had happened. The idea that someone else was going to move in and handle this.

Men like him didn't sit around doing nothing. The next forty-eight hours were going to be brutal.

# Chapter 6

Hunter was on his second set of push-ups when Emma awoke the next morning. He'd pulled his cargo pants over his boxer briefs but was bare-chested, and he didn't miss the way her eyes roamed over him as he stood up from his short workout and said, "Good morning." Or the blush that crept over her cheeks soon after.

Her full breasts bounced beneath his tee shirt as she sat up, her nipples showing through the soft cotton, and that silky red hair fell softly around her shoulders, framing her flushed face. She almost looked like the modern-day version of a Renaissance painting or something. Some sort of goddess come to life.

Except she was wearing far too much clothing.

"What are you doing?" she asked, looking from the rumpled bedding he'd tossed onto the chair to where he stood on the floor.

"PT. Sit-ups, push-ups, planks—nothing too spectacular. Usually I go for a run, but I left my running shoes back at the hotel. And I wasn't about to leave you alone here anyway."

"I didn't even hear you come in last night. I was so exhausted, I thought I'd lay down, and the next thing I knew it was already morning."

"You were already sound asleep by the time I got back, so I didn't wake you. It was a long day, and you needed your rest." His eyes skimmed appreciatively over her form again. His shirt was loose on her, but hell. It did little to hide her full breasts or her bare legs as she pushed the sheets back.

"So, what's the plan?" she asked, standing up. His tee-shirt was so long on her, it reached down to the middle of her creamy thighs. Just hanging there temptingly. To know her skimpy little thong panties were hanging in the bathroom had his cock hardening. She was completely naked beneath his shirt—and wouldn't he love to tug it off her right now and take her back to bed.

Convenient that there was one right there.

He tried not to stare at her legs as his gaze raked over her, but they were as stunningly sexy as the rest of her. All tempting curves and smooth, fair skin. And to know she was wearing nothing beneath it?

He cleared his throat.

Damn, she was beautiful first thing in the morning.

But he could keep his hands to himself.

"Are you hungry?" he asked.

He was hungry for a lot more than food, but that would have to wait.

"Starving, actually."

"Me too. I figured I'd better wait for you though, seeing as that the owners of the bed and breakfast think we're a couple and all."

"I assume you abandoned the car last night if you were gone for that long. How are we going to get back to London?"

"We're going to lie low for a couple of days," he said casually.

"A couple of days?" she asked, her voice rising. She crossed the room toward him, her breasts bouncing. Her green eyes sparking. "What are we supposed to do? Just stay here?"

"That's the plan. Maybe we can figure out what town is local and catch a cab there, but the police are all over this investigation. It's best that we stay out of sight."

"Oh, I'm sure you'll love that," she said, padding toward the bathroom. He could see the curve of her bottom beneath his shirt as she moved. One quick tug, and the globes of her cheeks would be exposed. He could caress his hand over her bare bottom, slide a little lower…

Damn it.

"It doesn't exactly sound like something you'd enjoy," she said.

"How do you figure that?" he asked, crossing the room and grabbing his tee shirt. Pretending her next-to-naked form wasn't driving him crazy. "Stuck in a hotel room with a beautiful woman? I've been worse places."

She poked her head back through the bathroom door. "You're a man of action—even I can see that. You were spending your time off working as a matter of fact. A little 'off-the-books' work I believe you called it? You couldn't even sit still for a minute. But waiting here in the middle of nowhere? I don't think so. Not doing anything for a couple of days while you watch out for me isn't exactly your cup of tea. And speaking of tea, I'd kill for some right now."

He raised an eyebrow, watching her in amusement. How she'd gone from him being a man of action to needing a cup of tea in one breath was mind-boggling. "They serve breakfast downstairs, princess. That's part of the whole 'bed-and-breakfast' thing I gather."

"Well thank heavens for that. How are we supposed to act anyway? Just walk down there holding hands, all lovey-dovey? Act like we're on a romantic holiday of sorts? You don't strike me as the type of man used to having a partner."

"A partner?"

"Girlfriend, boyfriend, spouse—whatever you fancy."

"I'm kind of developing a preference for feisty redheads," he said with a smirk. "But don't worry, I'm sure I can handle one breakfast."

She grabbed her bra and panties from the back of the door, letting them dangle from one delicate hand as she turned back to glance at him. "Whatever you say, sweet pea."

"Sweet pea?"

"Just practicing for breakfast. All part of the show."

He shook his head. "I think it's fair to say that no one has ever called me 'sweet pea' before, princess. Ever."

"Not your SEAL friends?" she asked innocently, a twinkle in her green eyes.

"My SEAL team, as a matter of fact, calls me Hunter. Or Hook."

"Hook?"

"Just my nickname. Every Navy SEAL has one."

"Because you like Captain Hook or something?" she joked.

"Right," he said, crossing the room toward where she stood in the bathroom doorway. "Who doesn't like him? But it might have more to do with the fact that I have a mean right hook."

"Well, I'll be sure to be on my best behavior," she said, turning back around.

His gaze dropped to the back of her thighs, and he muttered a curse. If he couldn't keep his hands off her for the next day, it was just part of the façade. Right. He'd just tell himself that enough times until he believed it.

"Get ready or do whatever the hell it is that takes women so long, then I'll shower and we can go grab breakfast."

"And I suppose you'll be ready in mere minutes."

"Yep. Unless you want me to join you in the shower."

Her face flushed, and he winked. "No worries, princess. I'm not sure we'd both fit in that ridiculous shower/tub combo anyway."

"Are you always this bossy?" she asked, wrinkling her nose.

He crossed his arms and gazed at her. Watched as her eyes trailed over the muscles in his arms. He didn't exactly mind if she stared at him—not in the slightest. "No. I'm even more bossy in bed."

She turned red and quickly shut the door without another word.

\*\*\*

Emma put on her lacy bra and thong before slipping into her jeans and sweater.

Good heavens.

No doubt Hunter had gotten an eyeful when he'd arrived back at their room last night. But what did she care? He'd been with tons of women, of that she was certain. So he'd seen her lingerie. It's not like they'd slept together or something—not even slept beside one another in the same bed. As she'd eyed him doing push-ups this morning, his biceps bulging and entire bare chest and back gleaming with sweat, she'd also noticed the rumpled blanket and pillow tossed onto the arm chair.

Of course, it would've completely freaked her out to wake up with a strange man in bed beside her. And as he'd already clarified yesterday, it was his job to look out for her. He'd literally been in the pub, listening to those men, because he'd thought she'd been kidnapped. Although she had no doubt he'd be up for a quickie if she were so inclined, that certainly wasn't her style.

No matter how attracted to him she might be.

Her gaze fell to a small vase of flowers in the corner of the bathroom, and she was reminded of the vases in the bazaar.

As soon as this whole mess was sorted, she needed to get in touch with her friend Lily. She was supposed to still be in Kabul, unless she'd headed home early to the U.S. after Emma had disappeared. What had become of the other aid workers when she'd vanished? Had they been frightened enough to leave the country and head home? Abandon their work?

Guilt flooded through her.

This entire situation was a bigger mess than she could have ever imagined.

She emerged from the bathroom a short time later dressed and ready to go. What exactly did Hunter expect? It's not like she had her makeup and toiletries with her.

"You were ready sooner than I expected," he said, jumping up from where he'd been doing planks on the floor.

"It's not like I packed for a weekend getaway," she said. "I have a few things in my backpack, and that's it. If we're really stuck here for a few days, the perhaps we should take a taxi into the nearest town."

"I'll buy you whatever I need."

Emma raised her eyebrows. "I'm perfectly capable of buying my own things."

"That you are. But not unless you have cash on you. Credit cards are traceable. So are ATM transactions. And as I already said, we're laying low for the next forty-eight hours."

Emma blew out a sigh of exasperation. "Fine. But I'll pay you back after this entire thing is sorted. And I do have some cash on me. Don't forget I just got back from traveling."

"I'm not sure they'll take afghanis here," he said, raising an eyebrow.

"I'm quite aware of that, thank you. Now if you'll hurry along, we can head down to breakfast. Sweet pea," she added at the end with a smirk.

Hunter muttered a curse but grabbed some clean clothes from his backpack. "Back in five," he said.

Emma did a double take a few minutes later when

he emerged from the bathroom. Freshly showered with damp hair and his facial hair trimmed, he cleaned up nicely.

Too nicely.

Hunter rubbed a hand over his whiskers, and she tried not to stare at the thick muscles on his arms. Or look at his broad shoulders and massive chest.

He looked like he could pick her up in his arms and whisk her away without even getting winded. Cover her body with his muscular frame and have her whimpering beneath him. She couldn't even imagine all that strength and power moving over her—inside her. He was aggressive and strong, yet careful. Controlled. She didn't feel threatened by his strength or power—if anything, it was the exact opposite.

She felt safe.

Secure.

And far too tempted any time he was close by.

"I was getting tired of the scruffier look," he said. "You kind of have to blend in with the locals sometimes though."

"Yes, I can imagine. It was a bit hard to hide my flaming red hair in Kabul. I had to wear a headscarf like all of the other women, of course, but with my pale skin and red hair, I'm afraid I stood out more than I would have liked."

"You'd stand out anywhere."

"Unfortunately, yes."

Hunter lightly grabbed her arm as she turned away, ducking low so that his lips were near her ear as he stood behind her. "I meant that as a compliment. In case you haven't noticed, I'm not exactly complaining about our current living situation. Hell, I can hardly keep my hands to myself around you. Not sure that I want to either."

She inhaled, her chest rising and falling as she felt his breath on her skin.

"Well," she said, swallowing.

Trying to ignore the heat rising inside her.

"I guess you'll just have to," she finally said. "Because this is strictly a short-term arrangement."

"That it is," he said in a low voice, picking up a strand of her long hair and gently running his fingers down it. He paused and repeated the action. She wanted to close her eyes and lean back into his strength. Relax into that massive chest. Let him run those big hands all over her body.

But that would be a mistake, because in two days' time, they'd part ways. Perhaps he did intend to bring her back to the States with him—but that certainly didn't mean anything. He wanted to protect her, and if she was honest with herself, she wanted to leave.

At least for a couple of weeks until some of this settled.

"Ladies first," he said, opening the door.

She faltered, then composed herself and walked out into the hallway. Pretended that he hadn't affected her so with a few words. Hunter grabbed her hand, much to her surprise, weaving his thick fingers between hers. Her arm rested against his muscled forearm, and she tried not to gasp in surprise. His skin was so warm. Such a contrast to the solid muscle beneath.

"Just playing the part," he said, his eyes bright with amusement as she looked up at him.

"Right," she said. "You're enjoying this far too much."

"That I am," he agreed.

"Aren't you cold walking around in tee-shirts all the time?" she asked.

"Nope. I run warm."

He greeted the older couple who ran the bed-and-breakfast, introducing Emma to them. To her utter shock, he pulled out a chair for her then asked if she wanted tea.

"Your boyfriend certainly knows his way to a Brit's heart already, doesn't he?" the woman laughed. "Do you drink tea or coffee?" she asked him.

"Coffee please, ma'am."

"Oh, come on," Emma teased. "Coffee? When in Rome—"

"Not a chance, sweetheart," Hunter said. "And Romans happen to like coffee."

He helped Emma sit down, brushing his lips against her cheek as she blushed furiously. His whiskers abraded her sensitive skin, and she tried to ignore the palpitations of her heart. Tried not to inhale his clean, spicy scent. His hand rested casually on her shoulder for a moment as he stood behind her, talking with the couple, and he absentmindedly massaged her tight muscles.

"I've been deployed all over the world," Hunter said. "Believe me when I say dirt would probably taste better than some of the bad cups of coffee I've had. Whatever you have will be great in comparison."

"Yanks don't really seem to like tea," the woman agreed.

"He's just like an American friend of mine," Emma said, trying to ignore Hunter's fingers rubbing over her shoulders and neck. "She couldn't fathom how I could drink tea every day."

"Don't worry dear," the woman said. "We have

both. And I must say, I wouldn't mind sending you room service tomorrow morning if you fancy," she said, smiling as she looked back and forth at the two of them. "Breakfast in bed? I'll just leave two trays outside your door. Give you two young lovebirds a bit of privacy."

"Wonderful," Hunter said with a grin as Emma flushed and said, "That's not necessary."

"Oh, it would be no trouble," the woman insisted.

"Thank you," Hunter said. "And everything looks wonderful."

The couple left them alone, insisting they let them know if they needed anything else.

"Breakfast in bed?" Emma asked. "Was that strictly necessary?"

"Just playing the part, ma'am," he said.

"Ma'am," she murmured. "Believe it or not, I may actually prefer 'princess.' Calling me 'ma'am' makes me think that you're talking to my mother," she said, watching in amazement as Hunter piled his plate high.

His gaze flicked toward hers. "I skipped dinner last night. A certain redhead caused me a bit of trouble, as I recall."

"Right. That was me shooting at you as we rushed through the hotel corridor," she whispered in irritation, selecting a few items to put on her own empty plate.

Hunter pulled his mobile from the pocket of his cargo pants, frowning, as he balanced his plateful of food in one hand.

"Is there a problem?" she asked.

"No problem," he said, slipping it back into his pocket.

"Well aren't you cryptic. The way you were glaring

at your mobile, I can only assume you aren't telling me everything."

"Just some info from my SEAL team," he said, carrying his place back to the table. Eggs, sausages, beans, tomatoes, and fried bread filled his plate, and he groaned in appreciation as he took his first bite.

Emma placed a scone, fruit, and some eggs on her own plate, then took a seat beside him.

"No wonder you're so small," Hunter said. "That's not a full meal."

"It is for me—you're nearly a foot taller than I am. If I ate what you did, I'd never fit into my clothes again."

He chuffed out a laugh. "You, walking around naked—I'm not sure I'd consider that a bad thing. Especially since we're staying in the same room."

"Very funny," she chastised. "I'm sure you chat up women all the time and take them home with you. But me? Never."

"You don't chat up women?"

"Oh never mind," she said.

"You're too easy to rile up," he said. "Must be that famous red-headed temper. Although I kind of enjoy how easy it is to make you blush."

"What can I say? The curse of being so fair-skinned. Oh, this tea is heavenly," she said, taking another sip. "I know what you're thinking," she added. "My friend Lily was amazed by how much tea I drank every day."

"I guess you don't have anything like iced tea here in England."

"Iced tea? No, definitely not."

"I figured as much," he said, taking another bite of his food. "I ordered a soda at the pub last night and they gave it to me without any ice."

"This isn't America," she pointed out. "There aren't 7-11's on every corner with massive drinks the size of an entire pitcher."

"It certainly isn't the U.S.—no ice in your drinks, you drive on the wrong side of the road, and you serve black pudding for breakfast."

"I notice you didn't try any."

"Not when I know why it's black. I'll eat damn near anything, but I don't think you could pay me to try that. I'd rather eat a damn MRE if I had to."

"What's that?"

"Meal ready to eat. It's a U.S. military thing. Tastes like cardboard, but they're loaded with calories. They're for out in the field—and trust me, there were times I was damn glad to have them. Nothing like pitching a tent in the middle of nowhere with nothing to eat. MRE's did what they were intended to."

"Sounds delicious," she said sarcastically. "A cardboard tasting meal loaded with calories and sodium I'm sure."

"Beggars can't be choosers."

"No, I'd imagine not. So, I don't suppose you can tell me anymore what's going on? You sent off the documents last night. I'd imagine your military has looked them over."

"That they have," Hunter agreed, taking a sip of his coffee. "I need to give my CO a call after we eat. Finalize some plans. But as you said, the information is out of your hands now. It was brave of you to grab those documents you found."

Emma shrugged. "It's what anyone would have done."

"I'm not sure just anyone would go sneaking into

Kabul on a visa they had no intention of actually using for legitimate purposes. Especially a single woman traveling alone to that part of the world."

"I've always loved to travel and had a flair for adventure I suppose. Archeology is interesting because I get to study new cultures, discover ancient worlds. And the aid workers I met were lovely. They were there for different reasons than me, certainly, but I'd have kept in touch with some of them later."

"Where's your American friend from?"

"I think somewhere outside of Washington, D.C. Not too far from you I'd imagine if you're in Virginia. Why, are you looking for me to set you up with a date when you return to the States?"

"No, I'm not looking for a date," he muttered. "I think I have my hands full with you at the moment, wouldn't you say?"

"Right. Sorry to be such trouble."

"No trouble," Hunter said, pulling his mobile from his pocket again. He glanced at the screen. "I need to make a call. Finish your breakfast, and then we'll see about going into whatever the closest town is. Getting some things."

"You're going to leave your fake girlfriend eating breakfast alone?" Emma teased. "Whatever will that sweet little couple think?"

"Yep. If anyone asks, just make up an excuse. Nature called."

"How lovely," she said sarcastically.

"Yes, you are," he agreed. "Tell them I'm calling my CO if you want—I already explained to them last night that I'm U.S. military. And that I whisked my lovely girlfriend away for a few days at a bed and breakfast."

"Hmmph. At least you still have contact with the outside world. You destroyed my phone if you recall."

"Just the SIM card—and believe me, neither of us wants to be tracked here. My connections are secure. It's safe for me to use my electronics. I'm afraid we can't take any chances with yours though."

"All right. Go off and save the world or do whatever it is you need to do."

"No saving the world. I'm stuck here with you, remember?"

"Right. Well, I'll see you later," she said, turning back to her breakfast.

Stuck here with her, she thought as he walked out of the dining area. How could she forget?

## Chapter 7

Hunter unlocked the door to their room, quietly shutting it behind him. He pulled his phone out from a pocket of his cargo pants and called Mason. His eyes fell on Emma's backpack, sitting beside his on the bed. Hell. The woman had been through the wringer in the past twelve hours—the past week. And the text he'd just gotten from Mason made his blood run cold.

"What happened?" he asked, his voice low. "I was in the middle of breakfast and didn't want to scare Emma."

"They went to her parents' house. Late last night. Busted down the door and demanded to know where she was."

"Damn it," Hunter said, pounding his fist against the door frame. "What happened? Are they okay?"

"Shaken up but unharmed, fortunately. The men after them were either affiliated with or part of the terror cell we were after ourselves. It seems that Emma's parents weren't even certain if she was back in the U.K. She'd called and left a brief message, but they had no idea she was back in London or that her apartment had been ransacked. As far as they understood, she was supposed to be on a six-month trip to Kabul. It seems that they have an alarm system on their house, so the men that broke in were gone fairly quickly."

"God damn it," Hunter said. "What if Emma had gone there? If they go anywhere near her, I swear—"

"Did she tell you she has family just outside of London?"

"Yeah, she mentioned it yesterday," he said, pacing the room. "She didn't want to go to her family or friends and get them involved in any of this though. And thank God for that. If she'd been there, they'd have taken her."

He briefly closed his eyes.

"How'd you find out about it?" he asked.

"The police contacted me this morning. They couldn't get a hold of Emma—guessing you had something to do with why her phone is off."

"Destroyed the SIM card," Hunter said. "She wasn't too happy about it either. She'd turned her phone off earlier in the day, but I saw her text a friend last night. I pulled it out right then and there. I'm taking her with me when I leave. They're going to be searching everywhere for her."

"I take it you passed on whatever info she'd found?"

"Yep, but it doesn't matter. She's seen it, so they want her."

"Now that the U.S. and British governments have

hold of it, they'll probably change their targets anyway," Mason pointed out. "The shouldn't still be chasing after her."

"Unless they don't realize she's turned over the information," Hunter said. "I can't imagine they'd keep tracking her like this if they knew she'd already shared it with the authorities. It doesn't add up."

"I suppose not. They don't know who you are or why you're together."

Hunter ground his teeth. "Maybe not. But it doesn't feel right leaving her behind. The CO wants me to stay with her for the next two days, but that's not going to be long enough for this to blow over."

"You just met her yesterday. You can't expect her to just agree to fly across an ocean with you."

"I dunno. Can't exactly leave her here either, can I?"

"Nope. I'm at Heathrow now—catching the flight you were originally supposed to be on. I have to board in a few minutes."

"Roger that. Have a safe trip back. I should be there in a few days."

"You'll protect her. And if you bring her here, the entire team will, Hook," he said, calling Hunter by his nickname.

"I know. Let's just hope it doesn't come to that."

He disconnected the call, quickly following up with one to his CO. A few minutes later, he heard a soft knock at the door.

"It's me," Emma said quietly.

Hunter opened the door, and she turned white as she saw his stricken face. "What happened?" she demanded. "Did they find out we were here?"

"No, we're safe. But you know the men after

you?" he asked as he closed the door. "Some of them went to your parents' house last night. They were looking for you."

"Oh my God," she whispered, her hands rising to her face. Tears coming to her eyes. "Oh my God. What happened? Were they hurt?"

Hunter's gut clenched as he pulled her to him, watching as a stray tear rolled down her cheek. His chest tightened, and he didn't want to examine that reaction too closely. He reached out and cupped her face gently, brushing her hair back with one hand and then wiping away the tear with his thumb. Hell. He didn't stand around wiping away women's tears. He wasn't usually around long enough to see any.

Wham, bam, thank you ma'am always had suited him just fine.

But Emma?

They hadn't even slept together. Had barely even touched. And his gut churned at the idea of any harm coming to her.

"They're fine," he said. "The men who broke in got spooked by an alarm system. I'm sure your parents were frightened, but it seems that the police got there almost immediately."

"I should call them, see how they are. Let them know that I'm okay."

"There will be time for that later," he assured her. "We can't risk it now. You could use my phone, but there's no telling if anyone is listening in on theirs. The line could be tapped."

"Right. I understand," she said, nodding as more tears rolled down her cheeks.

He cupped her chin, tilting her face up toward him. "I'm not leaving you here."

She nodded, and the look in her eyes nearly slayed him. He pulled her into his arms, holding the back of her head as she quietly cried against his chest. Let his arms tighten around her. He felt her breasts pressing against him, her small body trembling against his, and could smell the rose-scented shampoo in her hair. But this very second, all that mattered was her safety.

"Are you okay?" he asked a moment later as she looked up at him.

"I'll come with you," she said, wiping away a stray tear.

"Yeah?"

"Not just for me, but for my family and friends, too. If these guys are willing to go to these lengths to find me, then it's best I just leave for a while. Stay out of sight. If I'm not in London, then they can't very well find me, can they?"

"I'll have Mason get word to your family that you're all right. The police have been in contact with him anyway after the incidents at the pub and hotel. Hell, they'd be all over me right now too wanting a statement if they didn't know I was here protecting you."

"Right. Your job is to protect me."

"It's not a job—I was collecting info on those men. That was my job—not typically what a Navy SEAL would do, granted, but I happened to be in the right place at the right time. You quite literally walked right into my life—bumped right into me. But I care about you. I'm not leaving you here alone and scared while I just go back to my everyday life. Pretend this is over because I'm back on the other side of the ocean. That's why I want you to come back with me, not because it's some job or my duty."

"Oh."

He searched her gaze, then ducked to softly brush his lips against hers.

Her lips were soft, full. She tasted sweet, like strawberries or the ripest fruit. He felt her intake of breath as his hand slid to her waist, and then she was kissing him back. Yielding to him. Pulling him closer. Clinging to him like she needed him more than her next breath.

\*\*\*

Emma whimpered as Hunter moved his mouth over hers. He tasted delicious—all man and spice and the hint of the coffee he'd had earlier. His body towered above hers, dominating the room, shielding her from anything but his overwhelming presence.

She didn't—couldn't—make herself want him to stop. Not when she'd been scared and frightened and he'd protected her. Not when there had been chemistry sparking between them since the moment they'd bumped into one another at the pub last night. It was fast—it was quick.

But she was powerless to stop her feelings.

To stop him.

His hands slid to her waist, gripping her tightly, anchoring her to him. Her nails dug into the back of his shortly cropped hair as she pulled him closer still, and then he was lifting her. Holding her in his muscular arms as if she weighed nothing. Her legs wrapped around his waist, and she felt his thick erection beneath his cargo pants.

Felt him rubbing against her aching core.

"Bed," he murmured. "I'm taking you to bed."

In the next instant, he was lying her down. Following as his body hovered above hers. Pulling up her cashmere sweater as she frantically clawed at his tee-shirt, trying to strip him bare as well. She gave in and let him undress her first, lifting her arms as he pulled her sweater up and off. Tossed it back behind him.

His gaze fell to her lace-covered breasts, and he made a sound akin only to a growl.

Like a predator stalking his prey, he had her at his utter mercy.

And oh how there was no place she'd rather be.

"So fucking sexy," he said appreciatively.

His body hovered over hers, and a moment later he was kissing her. Sending waves of heat coursing through her entire body. His delicious mouth moved over hers like a man starved—like he'd waited forever to kiss her. And his unhurried pace was making her desperate for more of his touch.

He kissed his way down her neck, lightly grazing her with his teeth, and then he was ducking lower still. Palming one of her breasts in one large hand. He caressed and kneaded her as he gazed down in appreciation, running a thumb across her nipple as she gasped.

"I like that you're coming with me, because I don't like to share."

"Share?"

"I'm not leaving you here in London for other men to hit on. 'Chat up' as you say. I want this to be mine," he said, ducking lower and kissing her breast. Tugging the lace cups of her bra down so that she was bare to him.

His hot lips kissed her again and again, leaving her

breasts swollen and aching. Her chest rose and fell as she tried to catch her breath. Arousal dampened her folds, her clit throbbing, and she wanted his touch everywhere.

His warm mouth moved over her nipple, and she arched up, desperate to be closer. Suddenly her lace bra was gone, and he kissed her again, slowly. Sucked one nipple into his mouth and flicked his tongue over the aching bud, leaving her crying out at the sensation. At the shockwaves of pleasure rippling through her.

"And this is mine, too," he growled, laving attention on her other breast. He slowly licked her nipple, sending shivers racing down her spine as she needed more. More kisses, more touches—more everything. Her clit throbbed as he tongued her nipple again, and she moaned aloud. She needed him touching her intimately—filling the ache she had deep inside.

He traced around her areola with the tip of his tongue, then nipped at her. Tugged her nipple between his teeth. Blew gently to ease the sting of his touch.

His hand slid beneath her jeans and lace thong, and suddenly he was touching her intimately. Parting her swollen lips. Fingering her drenched pussy.

"And this is definitely mine," he growled. "Hell, you are so hot and wet."

"Hunter," she whimpered. "Please."

He removed her jeans and lacy thong, stuffing the latter into his pocket, and then he was parting her thighs as she trembled. He kissed her as his thick fingers trailed though her arousal-dampened folds, the scruff of his whiskers rubbing against her cheek.

The spicy scent of his cologne filled the heated air between them, and she was lost to him. Drowning in her desire for this man.

She ran her hands up his rippled abdomen, feeling the broad pectoral muscles on his chest. Grabbing on to his broad shoulders.

His fingers trailed through her sensitive folds, then circled her swollen clit as she cried out in pleasure. Hunter slid two thick fingers inside her tight channel, murmuring in approval as her inner walls clamped down tightly around him. He slowly thrust his fingers in and out, stretching her. Readying her for his intimate invasion. She moaned loudly as he scissored his fingers, stretching her even more.

He kissed her again, capturing her cries with his mouth, and then his tongue was parting her lips, thrusting into her mouth. Rubbing alongside her own tongue as he swallowed her mewls of pleasure.

He took one of her legs in his muscular arm, bending it at the knee as he pushed it up toward her shoulder, spreading her wider. His muscular arm pinned her leg in place as he held her open to him, and he fingered her pussy. Growled as she writhed and bucked beneath him.

Hunter's thumb slid over her clit as his fingers thrust in and out, and she clutched the quilt beneath her with both hands, closing her eyes as she began to see stars.

"Come for me," he commanded, working his fingers faster as he thrust in and out. Circling over her clit with his thumb with no intent on stopping.

The heat began to build within her, pushing her higher and higher. She felt like she was about to explode from pure pleasure, unable to stop the orgasm building within.

Her inner walls clamped down around him as his mouth claimed hers, and then she was screaming. Crying out his name. Surrendering to Hunter as she detonated.

He held here there, bringing her down from her explosive orgasm with a slowing of touches and softer kisses, gazing into her eyes as she slowly returned back to Earth.

He made quick work of stripping off his own clothing, and as she raked her gaze down his muscled abdomen, she saw his cock jutting out proudly before him. Pre-cum dripped from the swollen head, a bulging vein running down one side of his thick shaft.

He sheathed himself with a condom, and then he was gripping her behind the knees. Pushing her legs back as he spread her wide open.

Putting her aching, swollen sex on display to his gaze.

"Next time I'm going to taste you. But I need to be inside you right now. I want you too damn much."

He lined his erection up, and then he was filling her slowly. Completely. Penetrating her inch by painstaking inch, until the base of his cock rubbed against her still swollen clit. She gasped as he filled her, held her there. As she gave herself completely to him.

She couldn't move if she wanted to, and she loved this demanding, controlling side of him. Of the feeling she was spinning completely out of control.

She didn't have time to worry about the rest of her life—her entire existence hinged on this moment. This man.

He pulled out slightly, and then he began

thrusting. Holding her legs in place as claimed her, his eyes dark with arousal. His thick shaft filling her completely.

Her breasts bounced as he began thrusting harder, and he ducked down, taking one nipple into his mouth.

Emma was completely at Hunter's utter mercy—her legs spread wide, pinned in place as he held her open, her body surrendering to the exquisite pressure of his throbbing erection filling her again and again. His tongue flicked mercilessly over her nipple, and as the base of his erection rubbed against her swollen clit, she screamed.

Cried out his name as her orgasm went on and on. As she again was pushed over the precipice, helpless to her body's response to his touch. Hunter growled in approval, then stiffened slightly above her, thrusting twice more as he found his own release.

She lay panting and sated beneath him as he released her legs and slowly pulled free. He took off the condom and pulled her to him in bed. Held her close as she gasped for breath. His body was solid and warm, and she clung to him, letting him hold her as her head fell against his chest. Her leg draped over his, the springy hair on his legs tickling her skin, and then he kissed the top of her head.

Told her to sleep.

"Oh my God, Hunter," she murmured.

His hand trailed down her back, lightly caressing her skin as she relaxed against him. She sighed as she listened to the sound of his heartbeat and finally shut her eyes.

# Chapter 8

The sound of a car door slamming in the parking lot startled Hunter awake. He blinked, seeing Emma's red hair fanning across his chest. Feeling her curves tucked up against him. One of her slender legs was intertwined with his own, and her full breasts were pressed up against his side. He slid his hand down her back, allowing it to rest on her bare bottom. Loving the feel of her beside him.

She was so damn gorgeous nestled up against him, it practically hurt. There was just something right about having this woman here in bed with him. Normally he'd be happy to get up and be on his merry way after sex, but with her?

He craved more.

More of her cries as he pleasured her. More of his cock sinking deep into that hot, wet channel, right where he belonged. He needed more time to palm her full breasts, caress her soft skin, and let his lips and tongue thoroughly explore every square inch of her.

The bed and breakfast was otherwise quiet, but he heard footsteps crossing the gravel in the parking lot. The faint sound of voices. Emma's long hair tickled his bare chest as she stirred slightly in her sleep, and he reluctantly rolled her to the side so that she was lying beside him. Her bare breasts were so tempting, it was all he could do not to bend down and kiss her until she awoke.

Part her creamy thighs and enjoy round two and round three.

Instead, he tugged a blanket up over her and stood, grabbing his boxer briefs from where he'd discarded them earlier. He tugged them over his still semi-hard erection, groaning.

Worry niggled the back of his mind as he heard footsteps, and he pulled on his cargo pants, tucking his gun into the back of his waistband.

He grabbed his phone from the nightstand, where it had lay unnoticed while he and Emma had made love, and clenched his jaw at the multiple texts he'd gotten from Mason. He quickly thumbed through his texts, his gaze narrowing.

*Change of plans. I'm picking you up.*

*Flight leaves tonight.*

*Answer your damn phone.*

*Viper pinpointed your location. On my way.*

Hunter grumbled, running a hand through his cropped hair. What the fuck had happened while he'd fallen asleep? And why had his SEAL teammate Noah "Viper" Miller needed to track him down?

Every man on the team had an area they specialized in, and Viper was their computer whiz.

Mason handled their navigation in the field, and Hunter was the Delta SEAL team leader.

Shit.

He crossed to the window of the room, peering into the parking lot. There was only one additional vehicle there, and no one lingering around. A second later, there was a knock on the bedroom door. Hunter sauntered over, pulling it open and shooting Mason a look that could kill.

Mason's gaze didn't miss Emma's sleeping form on the bed, and he smirked. "Sorry to interrupt."

"What the hell is going on?" Hunter asked in a low voice.

"Good to see you, too," Mason said.

"Very funny, asshole. I thought you were already on a flight back home by now."

"Change of plans—we're heading out tonight. The shit really hit the fan when those men stormed into Emma's parents' home. It's all over the media—Emma's face as well. The CO thought it was better that we both got back right away, so I came to get you. And the Brits know you're watching Emma—they're on board with getting her out of the country."

"Spectacular," he said. "Let me get dressed."

"Yeah, looks like I may have interrupted something good," he said, clearing his throat. "Sorry about that."

"No need to be sorry," Hunter said.

He crossed the room and grabbed his tee shirt, then bent over Emma's sleeping form, holding the blanket in place to make sure she remained covered.

"Emma," he said quietly. "Time to wake up."

"What?" she asked sleepily, her gaze widening as she saw Mason hovering in the doorway. "What's going on?"

"Get ready. We're rolling out." He turned, then remembered he'd stuck her panties into his pocket. He grabbed the lacy thong and handed it back as Mason chuckled.

Emma turned ten shades of red.

"I'll wait outside," Mason said. "I can see you two need a minute."

"What's he doing here?" Emma asked, frantically scrambling for her clothes after Mason had shut the door. Hunter tried not to stare as she bent over the bed, plucking her discarded clothing from between the sheets. She turned away from him, pulling on her panties and bra, and he crossed over to her. Pulled her against him.

"We have to leave, but I'll keep you safe," he promised.

Unable to resist, he gently pushed some of her tousled hair away from her neck. Let his lips linger as he kissed her. With one arm wrapped securely around her slender waist, his other trailed lower, his hand cupping her sex. Her bare ass was perfectly on display in that sexy-as-fuck thong, and he wanted to curse at the God-awful timing of his SEAL team buddy's arrival.

His fingers explored Emma's sex teasingly, his knuckles running up and down her seam through the lace of her panties, and he enjoyed the little gasp of pleasure that escaped.

"Hunter," she said breathlessly, "we have to go. Your friend is right outside."

"He always did have bad timing," Hunter agreed, pushing away her panties as he fingered her folds. Her silken arousal coated his fingers, making him groan, and he slid higher, focusing all of his attention on her clit.

His other hand cupped her breast, holding her to him, and her circled her swollen nub, enjoying the sight of his hand in her panties. He worked against her more quickly, murmuring into her ear, and she exploded, gasping in pleasure as he held her to him.

Reluctantly, he let her pull away. Enjoyed the flush of pleasure on her cheeks.

"My God, Hunter. I can't even think straight when I'm around you."

"That's not a bad thing, gorgeous. I love hearing you cry out in pleasure."

She gazed at him, her mouth partway open in surprise, and he imagined her taking him into her mouth. Kneeling before him while he ran his hands through all that silky hair, and pleasuring him until he spilled his seed.

Nope.

Not gonna happen right now.

He watched in fascination as she shimmied into her tight jeans. Turned toward him in her lace bra. He reluctantly handed her the cashmere sweater and ducked in for a quick kiss before he stuffed the rest of his belongings into his backpack.

"I can't keep my hands off you," he said. "This is going to be the damn longest flight in history."

"What? Not a fan of the mile-high club?" she teased after she'd recovered from the orgasm he'd just given her, grabbing her own backpack.

"I'm 6'2"," he muttered. "I've never seen that as a problem before, but trying to cram the two of us into a tiny little airplane bathroom? No matter how small you are, princess, it's never gonna happen."

"We'll just have to wait until we're in the States then."

"It's going to be one uncomfortable flight."

Emma laughed. "Well at least we have a ride now," she said. "I was beginning to wonder how we'd get to the airport anyway—we can't exactly ring a taxi if we're trying to sneak around, now can we?"

"Maybe not," he said with a frown.

"What's wrong?"

"Mason said this is all over the media."

"Bloody hell," she muttered. "So we can't even sneak quietly out of the country?"

Hunter clenched his jaw. "We'll see. I guess we'll know more when we arrive at the airport. I'll feel better when we're back home."

"Right. I'll feel better when this entire incident is over."

\*\*\*

Emma glanced around in amazement as they walked down the ramp of the plane onto the tarmac the next morning, taking in the military planes lined up in neat rows and personnel in uniforms walking around. Hunter ducked down, saying he needed a quick word with someone, and hurried ahead of her. She watched him walk off, shoulders square, all business.

He certainly was a man used to being large and in charge, and my—how he'd done exactly that back in England.

She wanted to blush recalling the way he'd spread her legs wide, pinning her beneath him. She'd simply been his for the taking as he'd claimed her on the bed of the room they were staying in—and how she'd loved surrendering to him.

What exactly would happen now that they were here?

Hunter had insisted she stay with him, but it's not like she'd stay forever. They'd have a couple of weeks at best to get to know one another, and that would be it.

She'd go back to her life in London, and he'd go back to his career in the Navy. It was silly to pretend they meant anything to one another. She'd enjoy their time together now and then move on.

She'd never needed a serious relationship in the past, so there was no reason to wonder about one now. Not when an entire ocean separated them.

As she waited for Hunter to finish his conversation, she took a moment to simply stop and stare. The air blowing in from the nearby ocean was humid and warm—much more so than she expected in the Mid-Atlantic region of the U.S. The salty breeze blew through her hair, tousling it gently, and she closed her eyes briefly at the bright sun. Felt the warmth on her skin.

Someone had given her a U.S. Navy sweatshirt when they'd gotten onto a flight at Andrews Air Force Base after their jaunt across the pond, but she'd pulled it off the second she'd felt the warm sea air in Virginia.

It was the ocean of course, not a sea—they were right by the Atlantic.

Thousands of miles away from London—from home.

And thousands of miles away from the men tracking her.

Hunter grumbled beside her a minute later as they walked across the hangar toward the building. "I've got to come back to base after I drop you off," he said. "I was hoping to get you settled in, but unfortunately, this can't wait."

"Oh, right. I understand."

"I haven't been home for weeks," he muttered. "You don't have anything with you—clothes, necessities. There's no food at my place since I've been gone for so long. I'll see if I can have someone bring over some stuff for you."

"I know how to go shopping," she protested. "I've traveled extensively all over the world—I think I can handle finding what I need here in the U.S. I hear that they even speak English here—drive on the wrong side of the road, perhaps, but—"

She was cut off as Hunter growled and swung her up into his arms, leaving her laughing. "What I really want," he murmured quietly, "is to take you to bed. Not to head into base with the rest of my SEAL team."

"That does sound better," she agreed.

"And now that I've got you close," he teased, the edges of his fingers slipping beneath the back of her sweater, "I don't know if I can let you go."

"Put me down!" she said, glancing around. "Everyone's going to see us."

Hunter chuckled and righted her on her feet.

"I have no idea how long the debrief will take. My entire team has to be there, but the other SEAL team that's based out of Little Creek should be around. If not, they all have wives and girlfriends. I'm sure I can get one of them to drop off some things for you."

"Hook, glad you made it back!" his SEAL team

member Noah shouted out, walking toward them with a huge grin on his face. He was a couple of inches shorter than Hunter, but even bulkier. With his jet-black hair and massive muscles, Noah looked like he could intimidate anyone. He grinned at Emma though.

"And I've heard so much about you," he said.

"Save it," Hunter snapped.

"Whoa," Noah laughed, holding up his hands. "I figure any woman that can keep you in line is a good thing."

"It's a pleasure to meet you," Emma said, extending her hand.

"If Hunter gives you any trouble, let me know," Noah said, his dark eyes sparking with amusement as he shook her hand. "He may lead our SEAL team, but I can kick his ass if you need me to."

"Wonderful," Emma said. "With you and Mason around, it seems I don't need Hunter at all."

Hunter growled, pulling her toward him as Noah laughed.

"And speaking of Mason, where did he run off to anyway?" Emma asked.

Noah chuckled. "He got his girlfriend to meet him outside the gate—never seen a guy move so fast."

"I didn't realize he even had a girlfriend," Emma said.

"More like the flavor of the month," Hunter explained. "He went out with her once her twice—guess he thought he could take her home before we have to be back on base."

"Lovely," Emma murmured sarcastically.

"I guess he wasn't as lucky in London as you," Noah joked. "He didn't come back with a beautiful woman."

"Well don't I feel special," Emma said.

"Just ignore him," Hunter muttered.

Twenty minutes later, Hunter was grabbing both their backpacks from the trunk of Noah's car as Emma stood in front of his townhouse. "Debrief is in an hour. I hate to leave you right away, but that's life in the military sometimes. I'm lucky I had time to come back at all."

"Really, there's no need to worry," Emma insisted. "I'm safe here, and I can certainly occupy myself while you're gone."

"Right. Well, I need to grab a quick shower and change. I'll give you the brief tour of my place."

Emma walked around Hunter's townhouse, taking in the neat, modern kitchen and living room, then hesitating outside his bedroom. "You can stay here with me," Hunter said, eyes heating. "I have a guest room, but I want you here in my bed."

She blushed, pausing in the doorway.

"Hell, I wish I didn't have to go back to base," he groaned, crossing the room to her. He tipped her chin up and kissed her, then looked around ruefully. "I'd tell you to unpack, but I know you don't have anything. I'll give a buddy of mine a call—Ice. He's the leader of another SEAL team that's based out of Little Creek, but his fiancée Rebecca will get you sorted. Actually, they have a couple of kids, but she'll send someone over if she can't help."

"All right," she said, blowing out a breath as she sank down onto the edge of his bed.

"Are you okay?"

"Yeah, this is just all so overwhelming. I barely even made it back to London, and now here I am—

all the way on the other side of the Atlantic Ocean. In your bedroom!"

"Now that, I don't mind," he said, crouching down in front of her to meet her gaze. His hand rested on her thigh, and he squeezed gently. "It'll work out," he said. "I'll grab some clothes for you to change into. You can use the guest bathroom for now if you like. I need to take a quick shower, shave, and roll onto base, but there's a large bathtub in the other bathroom. I don't have any of that fancy rose-scented soap, but you can relax while I'm gone."

"After that long flight, a bath does sound nice," she agreed. "This jet lag has me really thrown off."

"Go ahead and get started; I'll grab some things. They say it's best to stay up and get used to the time change, but if you want to rest, go ahead. Can't promise I won't wake you up when I get back though," he said, winking as he stood up.

Emma padded down the hallway to the bathroom, seeing the dark circles under her eyes. Good heavens, she looked terrible. All this lack of sleep and moving around wasn't exactly helping. A long bath was exactly what she needed.

# Chapter 9

Hunter emerged from the shower and quickly toweled off, crossing the master bedroom toward his dresser. His reflection in the mirror showcased his bare torso—muscles, tats. Hell if pride hadn't filled his chest as Emma had practically gawked at him.

He worked damn hard in training though and didn't exactly mind the way she was attracted to him. His cock was half-hard just thinking about her, naked in the bath down the hall. He may have needed to be back on base ASAP, but a quickie suited him just fine.

Too bad she'd looked utterly exhausted though.

She'd been through a lot in a short amount of time and deserved some time to relax. Deserved more than a quick tumble between the sheets, too, he thought as he muttered a curse. He was used to charging into unknown situations, guns blazing. Deploying at a moment's notice. She may love to travel, but she was certainly in over her head this time.

Grumbling as he pulled on some clothes, he gave Ice a quick call.

"Heard you ran into a little trouble in London," Patrick said as he answered.

"That's an understatement," Hunter muttered. He heard kids screaming in the background and ran a hand over his jaw. Hell. How anyone had the patience for that, he'd never understand.

The noise quieted as he heard a door closing. "Just the kids," Patrick said.

Hunter chuckled. "Well hell. After hearing that, I bet you're happy to deploy all the time."

"Makes a difference when they're your own kids, your own family that you're leaving."

"Yeah, I can imagine," Hunter said. Patrick and Rebecca were engaged now, but when they'd first met, a stalker had been chasing after Rebecca. If anyone understood the situation of feeling helpless while someone was targeting your woman, it was Patrick.

And damn.

Since when was Emma his anyway?

"The CO said you ended up bringing the woman you were helping in London back with you," Patrick said.

"Yep. That's actually why I'm calling—I need a favor."

Hunter explained the circumstances, and Patrick said Rebecca would drop by to give Emma a hand. A busy lawyer, Rebecca worked full-time while she and Patrick wrangled the kids on the weekend. She'd know exactly where to take Emma shopping to buy whatever clothes or other items she needed.

"I appreciate it," Hunter said. "I've got to head

into base, debrief, and Emma literally has nothing but the clothes on her back."

"Give her my number," Patrick instructed. "Just in case she needs anything. She may be safe here, but that doesn't mean she'll feel comfortable with you gone."

"Thanks. Let's catch up over drinks sometime."

Patrick laughed. "I'm never at Anchors anymore," he said, referring to the popular bar along the Virginia Beach strand.

"Didn't think so," Hunter said. "Thanks again."

He hung up and finished gathering his things. Grabbing his backpack from the bed, he accidentally knocked Emma's leather one to the floor. She'd left it open, and some of the contents spilled out. He bent down and began to pick up her belongings, frowning as he spotted a gold band on the ground.

Picking it up between his thumb and forefinger, he stared at it in confusion.

This wasn't just any ring—and it's not like Emma was carrying around lots of jewelry with her anyway. He turned it over, noticing it had definitely been worn for a while. There were a few tiny, small nicks and scratches in the metal—something a jeweler could buff out.

And it was small. Feminine.

The wedding band would fit perfectly on one of Emma's slender fingers.

There weren't many reasons men took of their wedding ring—except when they were picking up women.

And people who were divorced didn't carry their wedding band around with them.

His stomach turned as he gazed at the gold band, a

sickening feeling rising inside him.

If there was one thing he couldn't stand, it was a liar.

He'd slept with a married woman.

***

"I'm heading out!" Hunter shouted as Emma soaked in the bathtub. She jumped and looked toward the bathroom door, expecting him to come in, but heard the front door slamming behind him.

What in the world?

Scowling, she climbed out of the bathtub herself, sloshing water all over the bathroom floor as she grabbed one of the extra towels. Hunter had said he'd bring her some clothes to change into, but from the sounds of it, he'd left in a hurry.

She walked down the hall to his bedroom, clutching the oversized towel around herself.

Stopping in shock, she saw the contents of her backpack spilled on the floor. Her mobile without its SIM card was there, her charger, wallet, and the small gold wedding band she wore when she traveled.

The one she hadn't needed for this trip, because she wasn't alone—she was with Hunter.

Bloody hell.

Is that why he'd shouted and run out the front door?

Because he thought she was married?

She nearly jumped in fright when the doorbell rang a moment later, and she looked out the bedroom window to see a car parked in the driveway of his townhome.

Sighing, she walked down the stairs wrapped in the

towel.

"Can I help you?" she asked politely.

The woman standing there smiled, her brown hair blowing in the slight breeze. "My husband is a friend of Hunter's—another SEAL. I'm Rebecca," she added, holding out her hand. "Hunter said you needed some things. I can see he meant that quite literally."

Emma glanced down at the towel wrapped around her, laughing.

"Yes, I suppose I do. Come on in."

"I brought over some of my own things for you to borrow," Rebecca said. "I can take you shopping if you like, but I thought you might like some things now if you needed a rest first."

"Right, thank you."

"You remind me of Patrick's sister," Rebecca said with a laugh. "Apparently, she answered the door in a towel, too, and nearly gave the CO a heart attack."

"The CO?"

"Commanding officer."

"Right, I do recall Hunter mentioning that. So he and your husband are on the same SEAL team?"

"No," Rebecca said. "Why don't I let you go change, and then I can answer any questions you have. I'm sure this—all of this—is quite overwhelming."

"Yes, that'd probably be best," Emma laughed. "And 'overwhelming' is an understatement. I'll be right back."

She emerged a few minutes later in a pair of cut-off jeans and borrowed tee-shirt. "I'd offer you something to drink," Emma said, "but apparently we don't have anything. So, er, can I get you a glass of water?"

"Water would be fine," Rebecca said.

Emma returned with two glasses of water and sank down onto the sofa in the living room by Rebecca. "So you were asking about the SEAL teams," Rebecca said. "Both are based out of Little Creek, but Patrick is the leader of the Alpha SEALs and Hunter leads the Delta team."

"Hunter's the leader of the team?"

"Afraid so. It's quite busy for them actually, as I'm sure you can probably imagine. They were all out on an op together recently when Patrick was injured."

"Oh my God, is he okay?" Emma asked.

"He is now, thankfully. I don't really know all the details of what happened, but I do know Hunter's team was there as well. They provided cover while Patrick was flown out."

"Wow. That's positively terrifying."

"It was," Rebecca agreed. "But that's their job. They train hard and fight harder. They're really protective, too—which I gather you already know since you're here."

"I'm afraid we've already had a bit of a misunderstanding though. Judging from the way Hunter blew out of here? I'm beginning to think coming was a mistake."

"What happened?"

"Oh, it's stupid, really. When I travel alone, I wear a fake wedding band—just to keep the strange men away."

"That's not stupid, that's smart," Rebecca said with a laugh.

"Maybe so, but I left it in my backpack. I'd just gotten back from Kabul and hadn't even unpacked everything yet. I mean, I was barely back in London a day before I was being chased. It looks like my backpack fell over in Hunter's bedroom, and he found it. The ring I mean. The next thing I knew, he was storming out. Slamming the front door. He didn't even stop to discuss it, just ran out."

"I'm sorry," Rebecca said.

Emma shrugged. "It was probably stupid to come here—I thought I was doing the right thing to get away. But I barely know Hunter. Flying across the ocean to stay with a man I barely know is somewhat ridiculous if you think about it."

"Maybe, maybe not. When you know it's right, you know."

Emma stood up. "Maybe so, but's it's not like we discussed anything. I mean, the plan was for me to come for a few weeks, but it seems like I foolishly rushed into this. I was frightened, yes, but I was also a little dumbstruck by Hunter. He's so big and brash and—I don't know. Not like any other man I've met."

"Do you want me to take you out now? Get your mind off things?"

"No, I think I'll take a raincheck. Thank you so much for letting me borrow a few things."

"Of course. I wrote down our number. Please give Patrick and me a call if you need anything. And let's get together soon, too. I'll introduce you to all the other girlfriends and wives. I think all of Hunter's team is single, but the men on my husband's team are all coupled up at this point."

"Wonderful. Thanks again," Emma said, closing the door as Rebecca left.

Uneasiness rolled over her as she walked back

toward Hunter's room. She could certainly understand why he'd be upset if she were married, but to automatically assume the worst? Slam the door without discussing anything?

She sighed, eyeing her backpack.

Coming here with Hunter had been a bad idea.

# Chapter 10

Hunter crossed his arms as he leaned against a desk in the bullpen on base, watching news footage on a massive TV screen in front of them. Mason and Noah stood to his left, Noah ribbing Mason about the women he'd left with earlier.

"Hey, she told me to give her a call when I was back," Mason laughed. "Who am I to ignore a woman's wishes?"

"Yeah, the minute your plane lands?" Noah said. "Have some dignity."

Mason shrugged, grinning. "I needed a ride and a quick lay. Nothing wrong with that."

Hunter muttered a curse as he strode across the room, taking a long pull from his water bottle. His CO was busy talking with two other members of his SEAL team, and he was ready to wrap this entire day up.

Only problem was, what was he supposed to do

with Emma when he got home?

His phone buzzed in his pocket, and he pulled it out, frowning at the message from Patrick on the screen.

*Emma's gone.*

Gone? How they hell could she be gone? They'd just gotten here for fuck's sake. As far as he knew, she was soaking her married self in his bathtub back home.

That's what he got for caring about a woman for a change.

Had he slept with a married woman before? Who the hell knew? That wouldn't have been his choice, but usually after a round between the sheets he was on his merry way.

He turned slightly away from the others and gave Patrick a call.

"What do you mean Emma's gone?"

"Rebecca was just over there. She brought some clothes and things for Emma. I guess she accidentally left her cell phone inside, so she turned around and drove back. Emma was getting into a cab—apparently she was telling Rebecca that coming here with you was a mistake."

"Damn right it was a mistake. Did she tell Rebecca she's married?" he asked, his voice rising.

Mason and Noah looked over at him, Mason's eyebrows raised. Hunter shook his head and walked out of the bullpen.

"She's not married," Patrick said. "She has a fake wedding band for when she travels—so assholes don't hit on her. I can't blame her with some of the places she goes. It's not safe for a single woman to be there alone."

"Damn it," Hunter muttered. "Well what does she mean that coming here was a mistake? I never even talked to her about it, I just left."

Patrick chuckled. "That was the mistake. She heard you slam the door and leave, and when she saw her backpack had been knocked over and the ring was on the ground, she put two and two together."

"I'll go find her," Hunter said. "I'll call the cab company or something," he grumbled. "I mean—God damn it."

He poked his head back into the bullpen. "There's an emergency with Emma," he said. "I have to go."

His CO nodded, and then Hunter was turning. Walking out the door.

He was just worried about her safety, he reasoned. She was alone in a foreign country. And then there was the whole terrorists after her bit. Perhaps they didn't know she was here in the States, but hell. He was worried because he needed to protect her, not because of the tightening he felt in his chest.

He grumbled, jogging out to the parking lot. Hopping into his vehicle.

He pounded his fist on the steering wheel in frustration.

***

Emma peered around the cab driver, watching the traffic ahead on the bridge. Cars creeped along, barely moving at all, and then when the cab she was riding in was finally over the glistening blue water, traffic came to an abrupt standstill.

She sighed in frustration as she saw a lone sailboat out on the water. The cars dotting the bridge stretched on as far as the eye could see—an endless stream of red brake lights.

Unfortunately for her, the closest decent-sized airport was all the way in Richmond—several hours away. A cab ride there was going to cost her a small fortune, but what was she supposed to do? Hunter's military connections had allowed them to fly in near Little Creek on a military jet from an air force base outside Washington, DC, but as for her?

She was on her own.

She'd swiped her credit card and purchased a ticket for a flight back. No sense in staying here with a man like that—someone so irritational he'd storm out without a civilized discussion.

Bloody hell.

"This is worse than traffic in London," she said. "There, in the most congested area at the city's center, cars aren't even allowed. It's buses and cabs only."

The cab driver eyed her in the rearview mirror. "Traffic's always bad on the bridge during nice weather. Everyone wants to head to the beach. People are always coming and going."

The beach. She'd never even made it there. Who came to Virginia Beach and didn't even see the ocean?

They were at standstill over some large river, but it wasn't the same as watching the waves crash on the shore. Too bad she hadn't decided to turn this into a holiday of sorts—check into a hotel and pretend she'd never met an irritable, irrational man like Hunter.

Although she could understand his anger at finding her decoy wedding band, the fact that he'd simply walked out, slamming the door behind him?

That he hadn't asked her about it or confronted her or bloody well done whatever a decent man would have?

She shuddered.

"You okay?" the cabbie asked.

"Yes, brilliant," she said, sinking back in her seat.

Good heavens, and she was still wearing Rebecca's clothing. She'd have to send her a check or something when she was back in England. Not that she knew her address or even her last name.

Emma blew out a sigh of exasperation.

The sun beaming in through the cab's window was hot and uncomfortable, and she closed her eyes, wishing she were stuck somewhere else.

The revving of a motorcycle engine startled her, and suddenly she saw two motorcycles pulling along beside them, one on each side of the vehicle. They'd woven through the traffic on the bridge and didn't remove their helmets as they stopped alongside her.

Her heart nearly stopped as she saw they were carrying weapons.

One pounded on the driver's sound window, shouting, while the second pulled at the back door where she was sitting.

"Go! Go!" she screamed to the driver.

"Lady, I can't go anywhere!"

The glass suddenly was smashed beside her, and she screamed as pieces of it rained down around her. A gloved hand reached in, unlocking the door, and then she was yanked from the vehicle as the cab driver yelled.

Emma stumbled as rough hands yanked her toward the motorcycle, and a hood was tossed over her head. In the next moment, a man bodily pulled her across his lap as he revved the engine, crushing her ribs as he pinned her to him.

She screamed as he revved the engine and began to drive, weaving in and out of the cars around them. Tears streamed down her cheeks as she gasped beneath the hood they'd thrown over her, and her stomach churned as they wove back and forth with her unable to see a thing. She could smell the acrid scent of old sweat and what had to have been urine.

As she cried out again, trying to gain enough balance to push herself away, something heavy thumped the top of her head.

Everything faded to blackness.

\*\*\*

Hunter muttered under his breath as he headed toward the bridge leading away from the Virginia Beach area. Of course Emma hadn't decided to take a nice holiday and check into a hotel on the beach—she'd booked a damn flight back to England.

He sped up, racing toward the bridge as he hung up with the cab company, cursing as he saw the multiple police cars racing by.

What in the hell had happened?

A couple of years ago there'd been a horrific accident on that very bridge. A car crash had killed a man who'd gone over the edge in the collision, and as it turned out, the man who'd died had been Rebecca's husband. She'd been widowed after the accident, and according to Patrick, was still nervous being over water now.

He didn't like the sight of the police and ambulances driving by, and his gut clenched as he pulled over to a police cruiser parked alongside the road.

"You won't get through for hours," the policeman said, his gaze flicking over Hunter's uniform. "There's been an emergency on the bridge. No way on or off right now."

"What happened?" he asked.

"Kidnapping," he said. "A woman was grabbed from a vehicle—seems she'd been targeted."

Hunter took a sharp breath as his gaze swept back toward the bridge up ahead. As he eyed the cars lined up, sunlight gleaming off the metal, and the boats bobbing up and down in the water below.

"Was she British?"

"I believe so. Why, do you know her?"

Hunter's heart pounded as he tried to think of the fastest way to get across the water. Call his CO? Run? Rustle up some favors and get someone to fly in with a damn helicopter?

"Fortunately, some state troopers were on the bridge and stopped them," the police officer said. "Pretty stupid to try a move like that in this kind of traffic over a goddamn bridge. What'd they think they were going to do to get away? Jump?"

Hunter blew out a breath he hadn't even realized he'd been holding.

"My girlfriend," Hunter explained. "We had a fight earlier, and she called a cab and took off for the airport in Richmond. She was, uh, involved in an incident back in London. There were men after her—I brought her here and—damn it! I should've been with her."

"What's her name?"

"Emma," he said. "Her name is Emma."

"It seems that she was shaken up but otherwise unharmed. There are police and medics tending to her now. You won't be able to get there unless you walk."

"Walk? I'll run the whole damn way."

Hunter pulled his car in front of the police officer, and then climbed out of his vehicle, anger roaring through him. He ignored the cars lining up beside him as traffic backed up even further and took off running.

A few heads turned to gawk at him from inside of their vehicles, but he didn't care.

All that mattered was getting to Emma.

He was halfway across before he finally spotted her.

She was sitting in the back of an ambulance, sobbing, as a medic took her blood pressure. A police officer was standing beside her with an open notepad, and four other officers had two men on the ground in handcuffs. He was tempted to go kick their asses himself, but right now all that mattered was her.

"Hunter," she gasped, watching in disbelief as he hurried over to her. "What are you doing here?"

"What do you mean what am I doing here?" he asked, crouching down in front of her. Feeling his gut clench at the tears running down her cheeks. "I came after you! Patrick told me you left, and I came to stop you from going to the airport. But holy hell—I never should've left you alone."

"I used a credit card to buy a ticket—I know that was stupid since they'd been tracking me, but I figured I was safe here."

"Are you okay?" he asked, reaching up to cup her face.

"I don't know—I just...you were mad and just left

before," she said, fresh tears rolling down her cheeks. "You didn't even try to talk to me—you just walked right out."

"I was angry, yes, and that was stupid on my part. I shouldn't have jumped to conclusions. I found something when your backpack spilled over—"

"The ring, I know. I saw it on the ground and realized what had happened. But you should have just come talked to me."

Hunter muttered a curse. "I hate that I wasn't there for you—that you ran away and those assholes tried to kidnap you again."

"But why are you here now?"

He took her hand, hating the way that it trembled. "Why am I here? Because I care about you. I came after you to stop you from flying back. And when the police just told me what happened? I left my car on the other side of the bridge and ran to get to you."

She burst into tears again, and Hunter pulled her into his arms. Held her tightly. Felt her entire body melt into his as he held her—exactly where she belonged.

"Come home with me," he murmured. "I made a mistake, but you flew across a damn ocean to stay with me. Let's not let one misunderstanding get in the way of that."

"Okay," she whispered, looking into his eyes. "Take me home."

# Epilogue

*One Month Later*

Emma looked around in surprise at the vases filled with roses in Hunter's bedroom, her purse falling to the ground. "What's all this for?" she asked.

"That damn rose-scented stuff you used at the bed-and-breakfast drove me crazy," he said, taking a step closer. Watching her with heated eyes. "Every time I smell the scent of roses now, I think of you."

"Hmm. That doesn't sound so terrible," she said with a smile, watching as he crossed his arms and gazed at her. The thick muscles of his biceps bulged, but she resisted the urge to run over to him. She wanted to see what game he was playing.

"Nope. Drives me damn crazy though."

"Is that so?" she teased, walking slowly toward him. Running her hands over his shirt to feel the solid muscles beneath.

He ducked lower and kissed her, tasting of man and spice, his hands wrapping around her waist. "And you know what I'm going to do about it?" he asked between kisses, backing her toward the bed.

"What's that?" she asked innocently.

"Drive you crazy," he growled. "Over and over again, all damn night."

She fell back onto the bed, and he kissed his way down her neck, palming her breasts beneath the sundress she had on. Kneading and caressing her. One large hand slid up her leg, and he was caressing her through her lace panties, making her gasp.

"Stay here with me," he said, kissing her once more.

"I am here with you."

"Don't go back to England. You've extended your visa, but I'm interested in making it something a little more permanent."

"How permanent?" she asked, gasping as his hand slipped beneath her panties and he found her aching clit. He traced in slow circles, teasing her, building her up, and she began to feel the heat rising within her.

Hunter tugged her panties down a moment later, pushing her dress up to her waist, and ducked down, kissing her intimately.

She gasped as his tongue trailed through her swollen folds, circling around her clit, and a few seconds later, she exploded, screaming out his name.

Hunter growled in approval, then moved back up her body, a gleam in his eyes.

"Stay here forever," he said, his blue eyes locking with hers.

She smiled, tears smarting her eyes as her breath caught. "Yes. Of course I'll stay here. I love you."

"I love you, too, princess."

He ducked lower and kissed her again as she surrendered to him once more.

## The End

# Author's Note

Thank you for reading Tempted by a SEAL, book eight in my Alpha SEAL series! This book features the first member of the Delta SEAL team, Hunter "Hook" Murdock. Hunter first appeared in the Alpha SEAL CO's story, Loved by a SEAL when the Delta and Alpha teams were sent on a mission together.

The series will continue with men from each of the teams woven in. We'll meet the new guys on the Delta team but see some of our old favorites as well!

As always, thanks again for joining me on this writing adventure. I wouldn't be here without my amazing readers.

XOXO,
Makenna

## About the Author

Makenna Jameison writes sizzling romantic suspense, including the addictive Alpha SEALs series. She is a #1 Amazon bestselling romance author. Makenna loves the beach, strong coffee, red wine, and traveling. She lives in Washington DC with her husband and two daughters.

Visit www.makennajameison.com to discover your next great read.

# Want to read more from MAKENNA JAMEISON?

# Keep reading for an exclusive excerpt from the ninth book in her Alpha SEALs series, *MARRIED TO A SEAL*.

Navy SEAL Patrick "Ice" Foster has devoted his life to the Navy, but when he met attorney Rebecca Mayes a year ago, she and her daughter instantly stole his heart. A surprise pregnancy means big changes are coming in their lives—and neither of them could be happier.

When Patrick's SEAL team is sent on a rescue mission to Afghanistan, an explosion changes everything in an instant. Patrick is gravely injured, and Rebecca doesn't know if he'll survive—or that he's already bought her a ring.

Patrick will do anything to make it back to Rebecca. But will the future they dreamed of never even have a chance to start?

# Chapter 1

Rebecca Mayes glanced out the window of her office Friday afternoon, looking at Virginia Beach and the sparkling waters of the Atlantic Ocean glistening in the distance. She brushed a lock of her brown, wavy hair back behind her ear and blew out a sigh. It was a perfect beginning-of-summer day, the kind that begged to be spent at the ocean, and she was stuck inside.

Along with the rest of the working world.

"Rebecca, are you ready to head to court?" her legal assistant asked, poking her head in the doorway.

"Yes, I'm coming in a minute," Rebecca said, gathering the papers and files spread out on her desk. "Let me just make sure I have everything." She stacked the folders into a neat pile and slipped them into her leather briefcase before pulling her long hair back into an intricate twist. She looked older and more professional with her hair pulled back, not that she had a problem holding her own in the courtroom.

"Just keeping you on schedule."

"And I appreciate it," Rebecca said as she stood. "As does the soon-to-be ex-Mrs. Miller."

Her assistant chuckled. "That bad, huh?"

Rebecca strode toward the door of her office, poised in her heels and skirt suit. "This is the case where they'd been married for twenty years and the husband cheated on her with their nineteen-year-old neighbor."

"Lovely. Exactly why I plan to never get married."

"Never say never."

"Easy for you to say when you've got a hunky Navy SEAL boyfriend who's utterly devoted to you."

Rebecca laughed. "Actually, I don't think either of us plans to get married again anytime soon. We're pretty happy with the way things are. Why rock the boat?"

"You've been spending too much time with Patrick and his Navy buddies," her assistant said, referring to Rebecca's boyfriend Navy SEAL Patrick "Ice" Foster and his SEAL team. "'Rock the boat?' Next you'll be telling me to drop and give you twenty push-ups."

"More like a hundred or so," Rebecca said with a laugh. "That SEAL training is brutal. I kind of prefer sticking to my office and the courtroom, thank you very much. Patrick and his team are out drilling on the water today anyway. And I could definitely do without the whole jumping out of helicopters into the ocean thing."

"I could go for a day at the beach—especially on a sunny Friday afternoon."

"Yeah, just another day of simulated water rescues.

They don't exactly relax on the sand like you or me—not that I consider chasing after Abby or Logan the least bit relaxing."

"Remind me never to have kids, either," her assistant chuckled. "I wouldn't mind working out with one of those SEALs though—in theory at least. I'm not going to pretend I could keep up with them. Or that I want to jump out of airplanes. But all that one-on-one attention with a smoking hot guy? A little mouth-to-mouth resuscitation? Too bad they're all taken."

Rebecca laughed. "The guys on Patrick's team are. But there are other military guys over at Little Creek. Even another SEAL team. I'll ask around—but I should warn you. Patrick's not really the type to do any sort of set-up."

"And do these single Navy men from base come to those infamous cookouts of yours?"

Rebecca glanced over at her assistant with a grin.

"Just asking for a friend of course."

"Of course," Rebecca said smoothly. "I'll keep you posted. Patrick does love hosting barbeques. And fortunately for you, summer is here."

"Not a bad time for weddings, either, if you don't mind my saying."

"Been there, done that. And Patrick has, too. We're over at each other's houses all the time anyway. Our kids are settled where they are—in their own house and school. I don't see that changing anytime soon."

"Well, you know what a wise attorney colleague once told me?"

"What's that?" Rebecca asked, absentmindedly digging her keys from her briefcase.

"Never say never."

Rebecca chuckled as she slid on her sunglasses. "Touché."

Ten minutes later Rebecca was driving along the highway in Virginia Beach toward the courthouse. She wasn't due in court for another hour but always preferred to arrive early to get her clients settled in and prepare for any last-minute problems.

Angry soon-to-be ex-husbands were known to roam the halls, attempting to intimidate their wives. Nothing like a contentious divorce to bring out someone's true colors.

She was proud of the cases she handled as a divorce attorney. Many of her clients were women, and although some just wanted out of their marriage without any good reason, there were plenty of women that she was really helping. Some were leaving husbands who'd cheated on them or hurt them. Some men just up and left their families without a word. It felt good to get her clients and any children they had what they deserved in the divorce settlements.

Although her own marriage to her first husband had been happy, not every relationship was.

She pulled up to a stoplight, glancing in the rearview mirror at the cars stopped behind her. Traffic always backed up along Atlantic Avenue in the gorgeous weather, especially at the start of the weekend, but she couldn't resist driving down by the water on this beautiful day. The scenic route to the courthouse it was.

It was hard to believe how much her life had changed recently. A single mom and a widow just over a year ago, she'd never expected to fall in love with someone again. And as an independent woman who was a successful attorney, she'd been surprised to be so attracted to an assertive, alpha male like Patrick. A man who commanded attention everywhere he went and no doubt had plenty of women fawning over him during his younger years.

He'd charmed her right from the start though—been protective of both her and her daughter. Tracked down a stalker set on revenge when one of her divorce cases had gone wrong. Been there anytime she'd needed him.

Throw that in with the inexplicable chemistry and draw they'd always had to one another?

Goodness.

She'd never stood a chance of resisting.

As a divorce attorney, she faced down fierce opponents in the courtroom every week. But none of them held a candle to him—six-foot-three inches of solid, muscular man. He led an elite SEAL team into battle and on secret missions all over the world. When those cool blue eyes met hers, though, she was lost. He was an aggressive, assertive Navy SEAL, but a caring father to his son. A protector to her and her daughter. An attentive lover.

And her boyfriend now.

She felt almost silly calling him that—she'd had a husband before and was thirty-one, not a silly teenage girl with a crush on a handsome military man. She had a house and a daughter, a career. But it's not like she could explain to her young daughter that Patrick was her lover, she thought as her cheeks flushed.

She couldn't even call or text him during the day like she did with her girlfriends—not when he was busy conducting drills out on the ocean with his SEAL team.

He had an entire career and life outside of their relationship—as did she.

It worked and suited them.

Her phone buzzed with an incoming text, and she glanced down to see a message from her best friend Alison.

Are we still on for drinks tonight? Virgin for me. Ugh.

Rebecca smiled. Alison was an ER nurse and was dating another man on the SEAL team, Evan "Flip" Jenkins. They'd recently moved in together, and she was pregnant with their first baby.

Rebecca speed-dialed her number as the light changed to green.

"Hi! Are you busy in the ER right now? I guess not or you wouldn't answer."

"No, hun, I'm on break. I thought you'd be in court this afternoon."

"On my way right now. The hearing isn't for another hour. I'm on Atlantic Avenue wishing I was at the beach instead of on my way to a courtroom."

"Ohhh, I'm insanely jealous. It looks gorgeous outside from the window of the cafeteria I'm currently sitting in."

Rebecca laughed. "I'm sitting in traffic, not on the beach. Aside from this, I've been stuck in the office all day."

"Tell me about it. I've had back-to-back patients in the ER. Something about gorgeous summer days seems to bring out the daredevils. So far we've had broken legs, broken arms, and a kid that fell off his bike and needed ten stitches. I need some kind of new career where you get to spend days like this outside. Evan said they're doing drills on the water today. Is it wrong to be envious of that?"

Rebecca coughed, trying to hide her laughter. "My legal assistant said the same thing—although I tried to explain that SEAL training isn't exactly like sitting on the beach with a cocktail in hand."

"And my days sitting and relaxing on the sand are numbered," Alison said wistfully. "I mean don't get me wrong, I'm thrilled about the baby. But sometimes a margarita in hand, chilling on the sand is exactly what you need."

"Amen," Rebecca agreed. "Those days are few and far between with kiddos. But hey, it just makes you appreciate it all that much more when you do get a break."

A loud beep from the background sounded over the phone, followed by a garbled announcement. "They're calling a code blue," Alison said. "I have to get back to the ER and see what new catastrophe awaits. See you tonight?"

"Yes, we're still on for drinks and dinner. I'll see you later on. And try to stay off your feet!"

"Easier said than done when you're rushing around an ER. All right, I'll see you later."

Rebecca said goodbye and disconnected the call, pulling into the court house parking lot a few minutes later. She blew out a breath, her wispy bangs fluttering in the air. A quick glance in the rearview mirror showed her hair had stayed back in the twist during her drive, so she grabbed her briefcase and opened the car door. Showtime.

***

Rebecca swirled the straw around in her iced tea

that evening from the outdoor patio of Alison's and her favorite seafood restaurant. Tourists walked down the sidewalk, loud music blared from cars passing by, and a block away, she could see the boardwalk and oceanfront. Families pushing strollers walked along, people leisurely peddled bicycles, and couples strolled hand-in-hand. She spotted a large group of teenagers laughing and joking, every once in a while pausing to take selfies or pictures of the ocean.

"You could've ordered an actual drink," Alison said, sipping her lemon water. "Just because I'm preggo doesn't mean you have to abstain from alcohol."

"I'm fine. I was actually a little tired earlier, so I could use the caffeine. We'll do drinks after the baby's here. Maybe even bring out some of the other women for a full-fledged girl's night."

"That sounds fantastic. Just a few more months!"

"It's getting close. Are you guys ready for the baby?"

"Ready as can be I guess. We've got the crib, stroller, and car seat. Not to mention a million teeny, tiny baby clothes. They're really cute, but I'm ready to ditch the maternity wear."

"God, Abby's only five, but it feels like a million years ago that I was pregnant with her."

"I'm not sure I'd want to relive this," Alison groaned. "I waddle rather than walk, none of my clothes fit, and my boobs are killing me."

Rebecca nearly spit out her iced tea as an older couple walking by their table did a double take, the elderly woman frowning and shaking her head in disbelief.

Alison shrugged and grinned. "I have to admit, I

don't mind Evan doting on me hand and foot though. After twelve-hour shifts in the ER, he's been amazing. Back rubs, foot rubs—and I'm telling you, pregnancy sex is off-the-charts."

Rebecca burst into laughter. "I guess I forgot about that part—the whole giving birth ordeal is mostly what's emblazed in my brain."

"Ugh—I'm dreading that. But I'm also totally ready not to be pregnant anymore, so…this kid's gotta come out of me somehow. With my luck, Evan will be deployed or something when the baby arrives. I guess it's a good thing I work in the ER."

The waitress came over to the table, and Rebecca ordered her favorite crab cakes. "Patrick's going to be late tonight since the guys were doing that water rescue simulation today. That probably means Abby will be bouncing off the walls when I get home later."

"Is your nanny watching her?"

"Yeah, and Logan, too. They went to McDonald's for an early dinner, so you know the kids are on cloud nine tonight."

"So both your kids are at your place with the nanny? Does that mean you finally gave Patrick a key?"

Rebecca flushed, feeling her cheeks turn pink. "That I did. He and Logan are over every weekend anyway. Plus Logan's been staying with us now when the team deploys. It's just easier this way."

"Mmm-hmm. Interesting. Patrick has a key and spends nearly every weekend at your place…."

"Nothing's changing. It just made sense to give him a key with us coming and going all weekend. What's Evan up to tonight?"

Alison grinned, evidently not at all fooled by

Rebecca's attempt to change the subject. "Not sure—he might go out with some of the other guys after training. I just told him I'd be home later than usual since we had dinner plans. He was worried I'd be too tired to meet up with you."

"He's sweet," Rebecca said. "And good for you. Those twelve-hour shifts of yours have to be grueling."

Alison's boyfriend Evan was the youngest man on the SEAL team. Although he was only a couple of years younger than Alison, she'd been reluctant to give him a chance when they'd first met. But now? It was hard to remember a time when they hadn't been together.

"Exactly how all the guys love to be described. Sweet. Nothing says big, bad Navy SEAL quite like that."

"It takes one to know one. Ha. I can't see Patrick going for that description either. He's more of the strong, silent type, and totally okay with everyone else thinking that as well."

"It works for him," Alison said, leaning back in her chair with a grin. "For you too, apparently."

"Who would've thunk it?" Rebecca joked. "Do you remember a year ago when we were eating out here, watching some of the guys head over to Anchors?" she asked, referring to the bar popular with the local military men and single women.

"All too well. I think I said I'd babysit for you or something crazy like that."

Rebecca burst into laughter. "You'll have your hands full soon enough. Plus, I think you said you'd babysit so I could go out and meet someone. As in go on a date. Since Patrick has a key to my place, I'm pretty sure we're past that point."

Alison snorted into her lemon water. "Just a bit." She leaned back in her chair and absentmindedly rubbed her belly. "But I'm pretty damn happy at the moment, so I sure can't complain."

"Let's go out on a double date next time—bring the guys with us."

"Sounds like a plan," Alison agreed. "But since they're not here right now, let me tell you about last night…."

<u>Now Available in Paperback!</u>

Made in the USA
Coppell, TX
09 June 2021

ROMANCE

# He vowed to protect her...
# but can he avoid falling for her?

British archeologist Emma Williams narrowly escaped being kidnapped while conducting research in the Middle East. Now she has critical documents a terrorist group is searching for—and they'll stop at nothing to track her down. The brash, bossy American Navy SEAL she meets in a pub was never supposed to be part of her escape plan—but if she can ignore his bulging muscles, bravado, and piercing blue eyes, she might just get out of this unscathed.

Navy SEAL Hunter "Hook" Murdock is on his way home from an operation when he finds himself tracking down terrorists in London. The feisty archeologist he meets in a pub isn't supposed to be the woman they're searching for—but he'll stop at nothing to protect her. The beautiful Emma may be book smart—but she completely naïve when it comes to her own safety. He'll watch her 24/7 if he has to—and attempt to ignore her feminine curves, pouty lips, and whip-smart personality.

When the Oxford-educated Emma meets the rough-and-tumble Navy SEAL, all bets are off. Sparks fly as they flee danger—and attempt not to fall for one another.

Tempted by a SEAL, a standalone novel, is Book 8 in the sizzling Alpha SEALs series.

WWW.MAKENNAJAMEISON.COM